Yellow Petals At Christmas

JENNIFER NICE

ISBN 978-1-912903-55-9

Cover design and typesetting by
Write into the Woods.

www.writeintothewoods.com

Books By
JENNIFER NICE

Christmas At The Manor:
Merry Christmas Eve Eve
That's It In A Nutcracker
All's Fair In Love And Christmas

**The Nice Romance Collection
(a series of standalone romances):**
Digging the Director
A Scottish Christmas Dream
Let's Skip This Christmas
Yellow Petals At Christmas

Join the
CLUB

Find all of the above books and sign up to the mailing
list for more at
www.writeintothewoods.com/romance

*For my mum, my dad,
and the dreamers.*

1

All of the black seemed wrong. Lillian had been all about colour. She'd worn a different colour every day, often multiple and clashing. In the summer, she'd dyed her grey hair and in the winter, she'd hidden it under a rainbow of hats.

Matt was stifled in his black mourning suit. He'd loosened the tie after the ceremony but was acutely aware of meeting Lillian's family and not wanting to appear disrespectful. At the last minute, on his way to the funeral, he'd slid a yellow rose into his front pocket. A lot of the ceremony had been spent sitting at the back, picking the thorns off the rose and wondering if he was bleeding through his white shirt.

She'd have liked the ceremony. A non-religious affair, her wicker coffin in front of a large crowd of friends and family, tears spilling onto cheeks as select people took it in turns to stand up at the front and share their memories. The lump in Matt's throat had grown, getting harder and harder to swallow on, until he'd been blinking back tears. Still, he hadn't cried. He hated crying at funerals.

They'd put flowers on her coffin before she'd been taken for cremation. Lillian loved flowers. There was a small garden at the back of the flat where she lived and she'd brought in men with machines to dig up the concrete someone had laid. The area had been turfed and a small patio created, and she would sit out there in the sunshine, sipping coffee. Around the lawn were flowers and pots, and more than once Matt had arrived at work to find flowers in his shop window that he certainly hadn't put there.

Not that he'd ever minded.

Lillian had owned the building, living upstairs from the shop, and she'd kept his rent cheap from the beginning. She'd even helped him out when he'd been lacking funds during his first year.

She'd believed in him, every step of the way.

It brought the lump back into his throat to think that now that she was gone, his shop might go too. Standing at the edge of the crowded room, he sipped his lemonade and spotted the obvious family members; the people others were giving condolences to. Did they look like the type of people who would raise his rent? Or worse, kick him out?

Matt needed a plan B, he needed an escape plan, but every time he'd tried to think of one, his mind froze. He didn't want a plan B, he never had. And anyway, Lillian had made promises. Promises that he was sure were in her will, because Lillian had always been a good person. The best person.

He could do nothing but wait, and maybe grease the way a little by somehow sucking up to the family. It was wrong to do it at the funeral, but when else would he see them?

Avoiding the family completely, Matt made his way to the buffet table and scanned the food, picking out bits and pieces, adding them to his plate.

'Ooh, cake.'

Matt flinched and glanced up, watching a woman around his age reach out for a square of the cake on offer. It was carrot cake and he'd avoided it as soon as he'd realised. Apparently, she didn't know. She reached out, frowned, gave the cake a curious look and then murmured, 'Ew, carrot cake. Why?'

Matt smiled and pointed to another cake.

'This one is coffee and walnut, Lillian's favourite.'

She followed where he was pointing and smiled.

'Thanks. Why do they have carrot cake? She'd spit that rubbish out.'

'Right?' Matt agreed, watching the woman's face as she scooped some cake onto her plate. There was no denying she was pretty. Her light brown hair gathered in a high ponytail, her green eyes flashing happily at the cake but tinged red and puffy from crying. She wore a black dress, blending in with everyone else, but over the top was a yellow cardigan.

She caught Matt staring and pointed at her cardigan with a fork.

'Yellow was her favourite colour.'

'I know,' said Matt, pointing at the rose in his lapel.

They smiled at one another, and it flittered across Matt's mind that you couldn't really ask a woman out at a funeral, but you could probably find a way to ask for her number.

He was still fumbling with this idea when she was called away and disappeared into the crowd of hungry mourners, lost in the sea of black and dullness that Lillian would have hated.

Sighing, Matt took his plate to the edge of the room, finding an empty seat next to a window where he could watch the proceedings, keeping an eye out for the pretty woman.

'What do you think, Lil?' he murmured. 'Everyone in black and serving carrot cake, huh?'

He could have sworn he heard Lillian's laugh, like a warm cackle lifting him up.

'Some family aren't chosen.'

The words were clear in Matt's head. That's what Lillian would have said, had she been there. But she wasn't. She was gone, and he'd never see her again. Matt was alone, hoping that this carrot cake choosing family would let him stay in the shop, that she'd done what she said she had, that he would survive without her.

'Not survive; thrive.'

'Yeah, yeah,' he murmured to himself, filling his mouth with a ham sandwich. 'Thrive. I hear you.' He sighed. Who was he kidding? Things were about to change completely, and most likely not for the better.

2

SEVEN MONTHS LATER

It was too chilly to stand on the pavement, looking up at the flat Lilah Montgomery now owned. The beginning of December was bringing with it a blast of wind from the Arctic, or perhaps the south-west coast of England was just colder than the south east. Not that Lilah had lived on the south-east coast. She'd never lived on the coast. The ocean and beaches were reserved for holidays, a week here and there spent in caravans and cottages, exploring rock pools and eating ice cream until it was time to return to normal life away from the water. Now, sandy beaches, crashing waves and ice cream would be her every day, even in the depths of the year.

Lilah grinned up at the flat's windows, her fingers rubbing over the keys in her pocket, passed to her by her mother just the day before. The building was a two-storey end terrace with a shop on the ground floor. Beside the large display window and entrance to the shop was the front door that led to the flat, and Lilah knew from experience that beyond the front door was a porch, a steep staircase and then a cosy two-bedroom flat. Her aunt had bought it in her thirties and opened a bookshop beneath the flat, until she retired and decided to rent the shop out.

Family holidays to this particular part of the coast involved staying with her aunt, sleeping on the floor surrounded by piles of books, and building sandcastles on the beach every morning. Unless they visited at Christmas, in which case there would be stories and marshmallows by the open fire in the living room and visiting a coffee shop along the seafront, battling the wind to get a hot chocolate.

The building was unchanged for the most part, other than a little more dirt and a few less flowers. Her aunt had always kept potted flowers in bloom around the front door and in window boxes attached to the flat's windowsills. The window boxes were now empty, the pots holding the last of the browning plants that Lillian had planted long ago. The light blue render was starting to come away in places, but the door was still in good condition. It was bright yellow with a small diamond-shaped window and a large knocker in the shape of a seashell. Lilah grinned at it, brushing her fingers over the brass seashell. Glancing to the side, she peered into the shop that lived beneath the flat. The lights were out but the streetlight above her flicked on just then, as dusk began to fill in the gaps between shadows. She could just make out the shelves inside and the counter missing a traditional till, covered in papers. The window display was enough to know what the shop sold. Low shelves were filled with action figures, books and small boxed games, while the bigger games and posters lined the back. Some of the action figures were big, in pristine boxes. Collector items, Lilah presumed. Posters by the shop door advertised a weekly Dungeons and Dragons evening and a Christmas charity quiz night at a local pub.

Pulling her keys from her pocket, Lilah pushed her new front door key into the lock of her aunt's door and turned it, pushing the door open. The porch was dark, the stairs up to the flat ever darker. Lilah fumbled for the light switch and for a moment worried there would be a shadow on the stairs.

The light flicked on revealing zero shadows.

There was a musty smell about the porch. Lilah made a mental note to give it a good clean and figure out a way of airing it without leaving the front door open too long. Moving all her belongings in would probably do that. Lilah climbed the stairs and pushed open the door at the top into the flat. She stood in the doorway a moment, taking it in. While her family had been in the flat in the last seven months, nothing had been moved, nothing had changed. The scent of Lillian Chancery filled the flat still, as if she was just in the kitchen making a cup of tea.

Tears pricked at Lilah's eyes as she walked through the living room, gazing over the worn orange sofa, the woven rainbow throw half over the back where Lillian would have pushed it aside as she stood. The rug in the middle of the room was equally colourful, a mixture of blues and greens, worn on the edge near the coffee table. A small television rested on a wooden stand in the corner, along with an old internet router switched off. Lilah wandered to the window and looked out at the view of the road beneath, giving her clear sight of anyone who might go into the shop below, of some rooftops and chimneys, and there, between the rooftops, a glint of the sea, disappearing fast into the dusk. Taking a deep breath, filling her nose with comforting memories, Lilah turned and investigated the kitchen. Her aunt's kettle and toaster sat on the worktop. The fridge freezer was empty, and Lilah bent to switch on the plug. When her aunt had left, knowing the end was coming, she had rid the flat of perishables and turned everything off. Everything but the power and water, making sure the heating would keep the pipes warm into the freezing months, should the inevitable take that long.

Before travelling that day, Lilah had made a list of the main things she needed to do upon moving in. The first was checking each room, in case any damage had occurred while the flat had been empty, although she was sure the person who ran the shop below would have let them know if anything had happened.

The kitchen was bland and cold, and Lilah had left her teabags in the car, so she moved on to the second bedroom. It was a small room with a window looking out to the back over the small garden and a parking space. Lilah's car sat in the parking space and the garden was overgrown. The sight made her chest tighten. Lillian would never have let it get that bad. She'd have to clear the garden and prepare it for winter, but first she'd have to look up how to do that.

The bathroom was musty but clean, the water still running from the taps when Lilah tried them, despite the pipes clanging a little. It was old fashioned, but Lilah didn't mind that. It would be fine after a good clean.

The main bedroom was a little bigger than the second, with a double bed, wardrobe and bedside table. A pile of books Lillian had been meaning to read sat on the bedside table, and the bed was made although Lilah's mother had long since changed the bedding.

Lilah sat on the foot of the bed and looked around.

'Hi, Auntie,' she murmured, glancing at her reflection in the mirror on the wall. 'I miss you. I miss you so much. And I can't tell you how grateful I am. I never once thought... I never even dreamed that you'd...' A lump formed in Lilah's throat and the words wouldn't come out without a sob and tears, which she wasn't ready for. Swallowing it all down, she reached back and picked up the book on the top of the pile. It was a romance set in a seaside town. Lilah smiled.

'Were you ever lonely, Lil?'

The flat was silent and that silence became almost too much to bear. She put the book back where she'd found it and returned to the living room. After a short sigh, she left to grab the few boxes she'd stuffed into her car. Emptying the flat would be hard work, first she had to decide what she was going to keep. Her parents said they'd come to help if she wanted, that she might need to hire a skip. Lilah wasn't sure about that. She wanted to go through Lillian's things slowly, to breathe them in, to understand why she possessed them, before she made a decision, and a skip felt too fast, too final.

It was a bit of a slog from the car to the flat and Lilah couldn't carry everything at once, so it took a while. By the time she'd brought three boxes, a rucksack and a big bag of clothes into the living room, she was breathing hard and covered in sweat. Now wasn't the time to stop, as such, but there was always time for a break. Always time for tea, as Lillian had been fond of saying.

Lilah pulled off her jumper, opened the window in each room to air the flat and then filled and put on the kettle. In one of the boxes were the few mugs that Lilah had come to own over the years. She pulled one out and put it next to the kettle, digging

11

through another box of provisions for the tea bags and milk.

'One cup of tea, maybe a biscuit,' she added, finding the chocolate digestives, 'and then we'll have a clean. Get rid of all this dust.'

The flat was still so quiet, its silence answering her each time, her voice too loud. Lilah's phone was in her pocket, digging into her stomach at inopportune moments, so she unlocked it and found the radio app, turning up the volume until music blared into the kitchen. She turned it down a little. While no one was downstairs, there was someone next door and she had no idea if they were in or how much they could hear. The last thing she wanted to do was introduce herself as the new noisy neighbour.

Lilah hummed to herself as she made and drank her tea, wandering through the flat, studying the artwork Lillian had up on the walls. She made mental lists of what she'd keep, what could go. What needed cleaning first, where she should start. Make the bed with her own bedding, put out her towels, give the bathroom a scrub, then the kitchen. She'd finish with a dust and vacuum of the whole flat. Then, she decided with a smile and a warmth that filled her chest, she would venture down to the seafront. She had no food for that evening, but there was a chip shop nearby and it had been too long since Lilah had walked along the beach, taking in the mood of the waves.

It was too cold for ice cream, everywhere would be shut, but the Christmas lights would be up by now.

Lilah had never cleaned so fast in her life. Soon she was pulling on her coat, quietly asking Lillian if she cared to join her, and closing her new front door behind her, locking it with a timid flourish. Lilah all but skipped down to the seafront. She had an hour or so before hunger would truly set in and she would stay out to watch the dark waves before taking a meal of fish and chips home with her.

Her new home, in this new town, ready for a new start and adventure. Lilah could hardly contain herself and gave a soft squeal, grinning as she stepped down onto the sand and let the sea air blow every negative thought away.

3

'So, you didn't get the flat?'

From his position, hunched over and face down on the table, Matt gave a loud groan.

'And you're *sure* she promised she'd leave it to you?'

'Yes!' Matt lifted his head. 'Well, not promised, I guess. More that she... But she said...' He sighed.

Danny tutted, shook his head and sipped his pint. Matt glared at him.

'It's all right for you. You have somewhere to live!'

'So do you!' Danny put his pint down and lowered himself to Matt's eye level. 'Go. Stay. With. Your. Parents.'

'I. Don't. Want. To,' said Matt, sighing again and poking his own pint glass, hoping it might magically go into his mouth without him having to sit up or lift anything.

'I don't see why not. Your parents are good people.'

'Yeah, to you. They disapprove of everything I do,' Matt muttered.

When Danny didn't respond, Matt glanced up at him. 'What?'

'What?' said Danny, bringing his pint back to his lips.

'No, what?' Matt sat up, watching his best friend since primary school, when they'd played football together on the first day.

'Nothing.'

'Danny, what?'

'I mean, you run a shop that barely has any customers and now you're living *in* the shop.' Danny quickly wiped his mouth, shaking his head. 'I'm not saying they're right. I'm really proud of you—'

'But they have a point, is that what you're saying?'

'Well, yeah, a little.'

Matt sighed and lowered himself back on the table, his chin on his hands.

'What do I do?'

'You mean besides—'

'Besides getting a proper job.'

Danny matched his sigh and looked around the pub.

'I don't know, mate.'

They sat in silence for a while, until Matt couldn't take it any longer.

'She said she'd give me the flat, Danny.'

'I know.'

'Why didn't she?'

'I don't know. Here, let's see the paperwork again.' Danny reached for the letters, partially trapped under Matt's arm and Matt released the sheaf of paper while somehow barely moving. Eventually, as Danny was reading it for the third time, Matt sat up and took three large gulps of his beer, feeling marginally better for it.

'I mean, maybe you just misunderstood. That seems the most likely thing,' Danny said, placing down the paperwork where it wouldn't get wet. He studied his friend. 'At least you got the shop. That's huge.'

It was huge. It was incredible. Matt Conrad was now the proud owner of his shop building. No more worrying about the new owner putting up the rent; no more rent. He owned property, something he never thought he'd be capable of. Yet here it was, in black and white, that Lillian Chancery had left him the shop she'd bought so many decades before and had rented out to him, promising she'd never increase the rent more than he could manage. In fact, on the bad months, she decreased it.

Matt missed Lillian more than he could put into words. There was a hole in his heart and another in his gut, not just because of her kindness, but because he'd never hear her laugh again. He'd never have to explain what something in his shop was again. She'd never be there again to bring him down a cup of coffee, to chat business, to buy him a sandwich for lunch as a surprise.

He didn't blame her for not leaving him the flat. She'd probably explained as much, but he'd heard what he wanted to. As he always did.

Matt put his head back on the table and groaned.

It wasn't Lillian's fault that he'd been evicted from his own flat, she didn't know he had nowhere to go. She'd been so ill, he hadn't wanted to burden her.

'Don't worry, Matty,' she'd told him the last time he saw her. 'I'm leaving it to you. You never have to worry again.'

She'd told him he could have her flat before, but now that he went over the memory, perhaps she had changed her mind. Perhaps she'd always only meant the shop. It was true; he never had to worry about the shop again. Other than paying the business rates, lighting, heating, water, internet... But the leasehold was now his. If he got really stuck, he could sell.

A small burp found its way out and Matt grimaced as his stomach turned.

Nothing other than fire and damnation would make him sell that shop. Not after what Lillian had done for him. He had to make this work.

He sat up with an exhale and gripped his pint.

'Okay, solutions,' he announced. 'What would you do?'

'Go stay with your parents,' Danny repeated.

'Other than that,' Matt said, swallowing fast on a mouthful of beer. 'Other than that, what would you do?'

Danny sighed, glancing at the time on his phone. Matt watched, the sudden burst of optimism draining as quickly as it had appeared.

'Well, you need money for rent, yes?'

'Not really, I need somewhere to rent first.'

'Hmm.'

That was the problem. There wasn't anywhere to rent. Their quaint town by the sea had been built by the Victorians, forgotten about for a long time and recently rediscovered by London's wealthy. They'd driven in like they owned the place and, pretty soon, they did own the place. Even the pub they were sitting in was now owned by two friends from London who'd dropped their well-paying finance jobs to live the dream serving craft beers by the sea.

Whereas Matt and Danny had grown up here, born in the nearest hospital, attended the town's schools, before Danny had left momentarily to go to university and Matt had made an attempt at a graphic design job. By the time Danny had his teaching career secured, Matt had decided to start again, this time with passion. When Danny's first child had been born, Matt had a shop and a rented flat. Life had been good, until it hadn't.

It seemed, all of a sudden, that Danny had the career, wife and family, while Matt was still stuck at phase one, fighting every day to keep his shop afloat. Now he was single and homeless. At least he still had his shop. And his looks.

Matt scoffed into his beer.

'What?' Danny asked, raising an amused eyebrow.

'Nothing. Just thinking that at least I'm more attractive than you.'

Danny laughed.

'Come on, you've got lots going for you. And now you're a property owner. Why don't you sell the shop?'

'No. And anyway, then what?'

'Take the business on the road. You don't need a shop for it. Go virtual.'

It was something Matt had considered, on and off, for years.

'No. Lillian gave me that shop.'

'Then rent it out.'

Matt stopped with his pint almost to his mouth. It would give him the extra income he needed to fight against other renters. But that still didn't fix the problem of where would he rent? The wealthy owned the flats now, other than the few still owned by the town's original residents, and they were let out to holiday makers for extortionate amounts. Those born and bred here didn't stand a chance.

'Where would I go? Don't say with my parents.'

'I don't know. Where do you want to go? The world would be your oyster. Go travelling. You know, you've never left this town.'

That was true, although Matt couldn't see the problem with it.

'Maybe I could split the shop,' he mused. 'So I could legally live in the back.'

'There you go. Problem solved,' said Danny. 'That was easy.'

Matt glared at him.

'None of this is easy.'

'You know life is hard, right?' Danny asked slowly with a sideways glance at his friend.

'It shouldn't be.'

'But it is. Do you know what it's like growing up as the only Black kid in the school?'

Matt puffed out his cheeks.

'Of course not.'

'Of course not,' Danny echoed. 'I do. But I don't know what it's like living in a shop I own. That's all you. Life is hard, Matty. Get over yourself.'

'Right, yeah, I'll do that. I'll finish this drink and let you get back home to your beautiful wife and your beautiful daughter and your other kid on the way and your glorious job and life. And I'll go back to my sleeping bag on the floor.'

Danny downed the last of his pint before mumbling, 'Teaching teenagers is not glorious, it's terrifying.'

Matt couldn't argue with that one.

'Well, you made that hard for yourself,' he pointed out. 'Could be teaching primary school, but no. You wanted a challenge.'

Matt and Danny looked at one another with narrowed eyes and both laughed. Matt clinked his glass against Danny's.

'Sorry, mate.'

'No, you're right. Look, if you ever need a sofa to crash on, there's one at my place. But you'll be sharing a bathroom with a four-year-old and a heavily pregnant woman.'

Matt pulled a face.

'I really appreciate that, thanks, but I'm okay.'

'Yeah, thought so. And hey, things will work out. You know, Lillian left you her shop for a reason, and I'll bet there's a reason she didn't leave you the flat. It's early days. Just give it a chance. Give her a chance. She always came through, right?'

'She did.' The gaping hole of grief reopened in Matt and he blinked back against his warming eyes. He lifted his pint glass. 'Thanks, Lillian. Best gift ever.'

Danny clinked his empty glass against Matt's.

'To Lillian,' he said softly, watching Matt down the last of his drink.

Matt had to open the shop the next morning, whether he felt like it or not, and Danny had to get to school before the kids, so they left relatively early and went their separate ways. The roads were narrow in this part of town, stretching into the old town, and only became narrower towards to the beach. Either side were old, colourful buildings, many a few centuries old, built by local fishermen. Most were now holiday lets.

Matt's shop was such a building, an end of a terrace built by the Victorians in the nineteenth century and pretty much left unchanged since then. A row of shops with large windows, and flats over the top. The road had been cobbled once – Lillian had shown Matt an old photograph – but the council, in its infinite wisdom, had paved over the cobbles to save the tyres of modern cars which squeezed down during the summer. Fumbling for his keys, he daren't look up at Lillian's old flat. The flat that should have been his. What if her ghost was staring back at him? Instead, he kept his eyes down and let himself into his shop, the bell above the door ringing sadly in the darkness. He locked the door behind him and turned to face his life's work. The carpet was threadbare, but the walls were bright, even in the gloom. The shelves were full of stock and the counter held his notebook full of stock takings and doodles, and, underneath, a hidden, locked compartment for his laptop. Behind was a stool and a mini fridge just for him. It sang with promise, even in the empty silence.

He left the lights off and wandered around the shelves, towards the back of the shop. Finding the key, he unlocked the staff door to the back room and revealed a small kitchenette with his sleeping bag on the floor. The sleeping bag was surrounded by boxes, except for one side where there was a sink, a cupboard and a small worktop holding a kettle, two mugs, one plate and a packet of biscuits. He used the toilet next door first, splashing water on his face and brushing his teeth, avoiding his reflection in the mirror. Then he settled in his sleeping bag and thought about the idea of renting the shop out to someone else. Where would he keep his stock? Currently it was in boxes around him, in the tiny kitchenette, but most of it was on the shelves in the shop. He'd need to buy a van, he supposed, and keep it in there. Maybe one of those converted vans so he could live it in too.

Matt frowned. What was the difference between that and sleeping in his shop? Other than the wheels. That led him back to the alternative route of converting the back of the shop into a residential area. He'd need planning permission and trades-people, and to make his shop floor smaller, but in theory it was doable. Perfectly doable, with a bit of financial help, maybe with a loan from the bank. Another loan. Matt's eyes were drifting shut, thanks to the beer rather than the anxiety, but they snapped open when a sound came from above his head.

It was all right. Just Lillian moving around.

Except that Lillian had died months ago. Matt sat up and listened. Who was moving around in her flat? Was she being burgled?

He listened carefully, staring down at his sleeping bag, until his gaze drifted over the paperwork for his shop.

'Oh,' he murmured. It wasn't Lillian, or a burglar. It was the flat's new owner. They must have gotten the keys, just as Matt had received his paperwork. 'Great.' He lay back down, listening for more noise. 'Can't wait to meet them,' he grumbled. There came no more noise and soon Matt was snoring softly, unaware of the corner of his sleeping bag moving ever so slightly, as if in an attempt to cover him and keep him warm.

It was dull and grey at half nine when Lilah opened her front door and stepped out. Or at least she attempted to step out. The wind immediately pushed her back in. She gave an *oof* and tried again, bracing herself. It wasn't raining, not yet, but the clouds hung heavy over the town and the wind was what her father would call 'bracing'. She managed to close her front door behind her without slamming it, locked it, pushed the keys into her pocket and faced the road, all the time with her eyes narrowed against any debris that might be blown into her. The plants, either side of the front door, were taking a bashing but Lilah guessed they'd been through worse. Unless Lillian had always brought them in during the winter. She considered unlocking the front door and how heavy those pots might be to drag inside, what creatures were lurking beneath that she might disturb or invite into her home.

The plants had to realise that Lillian was gone,

and Lilah was probably not who they'd like as their custodian. She'd never been good with plants. Still, she vowed to try bringing them inside when she returned home. Or maybe later. Tomorrow, when the wind had died down. Eventually. She'd bring them inside eventually. She had plenty of time before the first frost.

Lilah had no idea when the frosts started, but she ignored this fact and stepped out to the road, straight into the wind and was forced back to her front door.

'I'm going out,' she told the wind. 'You can't stop me.'

Off to her right, the shop was still dark inside. Nothing had moved, there was no sign of life. That made sense. It was the off season and it seemed like the type of shop that would only open during the touristy season in summer. At least she didn't have to meet her immediate neighbour just yet. There would be talk of Lillian, given that she'd owned the shop and left it to the current tenant, now owner, and Lilah wasn't quite ready for that. She'd thought she was, gearing herself up for the talk as she'd walked down the stairs to the front door, on the off chance that she bumped into the shop owner as she stepped out. To find the shop in darkness was a relief.

'Third time's the charm,' Lilah told herself, once again stepping out to the road. This time she managed to walk away from her flat, cross the road and head towards the beach. Each step was an effort, fighting against the wind, holding her bag close to her. Maybe this had been a bad idea, but she had to start some time, and the alternative was staying inside sorting through Lillian's things. That was this afternoon's job. First, Lilah wanted to be out in the world.

She made it to the end of the road, turned right so that she was buffeted by the wind from the side, then turned left so it was hitting her in the face again. By the time she made it to the promenade, her eyes were blurry with protective tears and her cheeks stung.

Unlit Christmas decorations surrounded her. Above her, between the shops, were lights ready to turn on and small Christmas trees in pots being battered by the wind. Lilah hoped they wouldn't be too damaged, assuring herself the town council knew what they were doing.

The beach was deserted. An expanse of wet yellow sand leading down to the tide that was half in, or half out depending on your mood. The waves that hit the sand were furious and large, beating the beach with every push forward and echoing the roar of the wind. It was harsh and uninviting, and yet it filled Lilah with joy. Her chest full to bursting, she grinned at the ocean, the grief inside her welling along with the waves.

She stumbled along the front, passing closed ice cream huts and shops that usually sold hats and buckets and spades, and found an inlet, sheltered from the wind. Inside were benches and on those benches were a few elderly couples, staring out to sea, and a woman with wild silver hair, held back in a tartan bandana, sitting in front of an easel.

Lilah sat away from everyone and watched the woman as subtly as possible. She was using oils to paint the anger of the ocean, dabs of grey and blue and white. It was beautiful, and Lilah felt almost stupid, opening her bag and pulling out a sketch-book.

She'd found the sketchbook at an art fair the year before, just as things were starting to go wrong, and had been compelled to buy it. She didn't own any pencils, let alone anything else to sketch or paint with, but she'd kept the sketchbook through it all.

The previous night, going through Lillian's things in the bedroom, a box had pretty much fallen on her from the top of a wardrobe, a box marked 'ART'. Opening it with trepidation, Lilah had found paints and pencils and sketchbooks filled with Lillian's art. They were often rough and some had been scribbled through with frustration, but all of them were so full of emotion that Lilah's head had begun to spin as she turned the pages.

Quite a few of the paintings had been of this view, sitting here sheltered from the weather, look-ing out across the beach to the sea. In all weathers, in all seasons, in oils and charcoal and water-colours.

Lilah had laid on the sofa that evening, sipping from a glass of wine, and made the decision to continue what Lillian had started. It seemed as good a place as any to start, given what Lilah wanted her new life to be. She'd packed her untouched sketchbook and Lillian's watercolour set, along with a fine paintbrush and a small water pot with a screwed on lid that had also been in the box, and determined to start the day painting the sea.

And here she was, sitting perhaps where Lillian had sat so many times, looking out at the same view, with some of the same paints. Lilah did her best to set herself up on the bench. She didn't have an easel, so lay the sketchbook on her lap. The pot of water and watercolours lay on the bench beside her, and Lilah stared down at the blank page, and then up at the view. Then back at the blank page.

Biting her lip, Lilah dipped the paintbrush into the water and went back to staring.

'First time?'

She jumped, the sketchbook sliding from her lap. She saved it just before it fell. Looking up, she found the painter smiling over at her.

'Oh, yes.'

The woman gave her an encouraging smile.

'Don't think about it too much.'

Lilah nodded, glancing to the woman's painting.

'Yours is amazing.'

'Thank you. I paint most mornings.'

'I'd love to do that. I just moved here. My aunt died and left me her house and belongings and these watercolours were on top of her wardrobe with her sketchbooks. They're all full of her paintings of this view and I just wanted... I mean, I wanted to before I moved here, it's like she knew, but...' Lilah sighed and stared out at the angry sea, tears welling up in her eyes. She blinked them back. Now was not the time nor the place.

The woman was studying her, her large hoop earrings swaying in the wind and with the movement of her breath.

'Your aunt wasn't Lillian, was she?'

Startled, Lilah turned back to her.

'You knew her?'

'Of course. I recognise her watercolours, there. She painted her initials on the lid, see? She came here often to paint. We'd go for coffee afterwards. We had a stall together at the art fairs sometimes.' The woman smiled. 'I miss her so much I want to scream into the waves,' she added quietly.

Lilah swallowed on a hard lump in her throat.

'I'm Lilah.'

The woman beamed.

'Were you named after her?'

Lilah nodded.

'Bea.' Bea held out a hand, bracelets jangling on her wrist as her coat sleeve moved up, and Lilah shook it awkwardly at an angle. 'So lovely to meet you.'

'And you.' Lilah glanced down at her blank page again. 'Where do you start?' she asked, a single tear escaping and dropping down her cheek.

Bea leaned over to look at Lilah's empty page, her watercolours and then her view. Her scent of cinnamon, vanilla and sea salt filled Lilah's world for a moment, although the sea salt could have just been on the wind.

'With watercolours, you can start with a wash. I'd put the base colours in, the sea, sky and sand. Let them blend a little if you want. Experiment. Then, when it's dry, which won't take long in this wind, add in the details.'

Lilah frowned a little, lifting her paintbrush.

'Don't think too hard about it,' Bea reminded her. 'Just go with what feels right. Play with it.'

'Right. Thank you. Play with it.' Lilah flashed Bea a smile and they both turned back to their paintings.

Lilah wet her brush again and wet the page, then moved the brush over the blue paint. It went on the page light, spreading over the water base. It was too light, so Lilah tried some black, which was too dark. She added some white and then some green, letting the wet paint mix on the page. Satisfied, she looked up at the sky and wondered if she should wait for her sea base to dry first. She should have started with the sky.

'Have you taken any classes?' Bea asked gently, her brush moving easily across her canvas.

'Not for a long time. I keep meaning to find a class, but something inside me just wants to get on with it.'

'I know what you mean,' said Bea, smiling as she washed her brush. 'The urge to put something onto paper. To create.' She glanced at Lilah. 'You don't need to do any classes if you don't want to.'

'Are there any local ones?'

'Oh, yes. I'm happy to recommend a couple.'

'Thanks. I'd appreciate that.'

'But don't feel you have to go.' Bea studied her a moment. 'Where have you moved here from?'

'Near London,' said Lilah, putting white and a hint of black at the top of her page, trying to emulate the dark, brooding sky.

'Do you still work there?'

'No. I was made redundant a year ago and haven't been able to get a new permanent job since. The market isn't great, especially in my industry, so I've been temping as admin.'

'What's your industry?'

'Design, at first, then I somehow moved into digital marketing.'

Bea gave Lilah a blank look.

'Exactly,' said Lilah. 'Then the machines came and the agency decided to cut some staff. I thought it would be for the best. Agency life is hard and fast, you never get a moment's peace. But I couldn't get another design job at all.'

'Are you job hunting here? I can't imagine the

job market is better here.'

Lilah smiled.

'Actually, I was hoping to take some time out and become an artist.' She glanced at Bea. 'I know that sounds stupid. But I have savings and what Lillian left me, and I thought if I don't try now, then when?'

'When you're retired and running out of time,' Bea confirmed. 'And you'll wish you'd started earlier. Good for you. Lilly would be proud.'

Lilah beamed, new tears pricking at her eyes.

'Thanks. You don't think it's stupid? I haven't done much since my teens. I used to be quite good. But then I had to go get a proper job and pay bills, and the art sort of got left behind.'

Bea shrugged, turning back to her painting.

'Art doesn't die inside you. It can just get really small. It comes out with practice, that's all. You're obviously creative, you're feeling things right now, it sounds like the best time to make the art inside you big again.'

Lilah's chest swelled with pride and hope. She nodded, biting her lip hard to stop more tears, and Bea gave her a sweet smile.

'How about after this, we go get a coffee and cake? Warm ourselves up?'

'That would be lovely,' said Lilah with surprise. 'Thank you. I'm guessing you waited until you retired to start your art?'

'I did. For a long time I was too busy raising

children and working to keep a roof over our heads. Now it's just me, my equally retired husband, our cat and the pension I've worked so hard for.'

'So, you've earned it.'

Bea glanced at her.

'It's stupid to earn it that way,' she told Lilah. 'If you want something, you must grab it. Depending on the situation, of course.'

'Of course.'

'Can't go around grabbing crabs.'

Lilah gave Bea a startled look.

'On the beach.' Bea gestured to their view.

'Oh. Right. No. Nope, can't do that.'

'But opportunities and the things that bring you joy? Those are the things you grab. Because you never know...'

'You never know,' Lilah agreed.

Neither of them finished the sentence, but it hung in the air between them anyway. *You never know how long you have left*.

They painted to the sound of the wind and waves until they both grew too cold to continue, and as they painted, an empty space sat between them, listening to their conversations, watching their brush strokes.

5

The alarm beeped at the same rhythm as his pounding head. Matt groaned and felt around for his phone without opening his eyes. In the end, the beeping became too insistent and Matt was forced to open his eyes and wake up. He turned off the alarm with a heavy finger and lay back in his sleeping bag, staring up at the ceiling. The ceiling of his own shop. His own ceiling. He frowned, wondering if it needed painting, before deciding against it and sighing hard. Matt sat up and ran his hands over his face and through his brown ruffled hair that was, as his mother regularly reminded him, in desperate need of a cut. Its length and style suited him just fine.

The beeping alarm may have stopped, but the pounding head hadn't. He hadn't drunk that much the night before, since when had hangovers come across him this easily? He certainly shouldn't have downed the last half as he and Danny were leaving the pub. He hadn't been drunk, but the older he got the less that seemed to matter.

Dragging himself to his feet, Matt groaned, stretching out his back before rolling up his sleeping bag and shoving it in the corner. He couldn't do this for long. He had to find somewhere else to live. With a deep sigh, he looked up at the ceiling again, wishing upon wish that he owned the flat along with the shop. It had seemed too good to be true when Lillian had told him she would take care of him, she wouldn't let him suffer when she died. Of course she hadn't left him the flat. Lillian had family. They'd use it as a holiday home or something. Even if they put it on the market, he would never be able to afford it.

Another sigh and Matt looked around the small room at the back of his shop. He could sell up. Pocket the money and move away, go travelling, sell his wares through Amazon warehouses so he didn't have to do anything. Or he could buy a van and convert it. He'd seen people doing that on social media, it didn't look so hard. Not until you started to really think about it. How did you get electricity and running water in a van?

Shaking his head, Matt went into the small toilet next door, brushed his teeth and splashed water on his face, before finding his deodorant and a clean t-shirt. Eventually, he would come up with an idea that worked. But it probably wouldn't be today.

One more sigh and Matt looked up at the ceiling again, wiping his wet neck with a towel, wondering if whoever was up there now would mind him using the shower. Looking around, he wondered again if he could convert the back of the shop into a residential area. Where would the bathroom go? It would have to be a studio flat-style arrangement. That would be better than nothing. It was the expense that was the problem. Surely if he could afford to do that, he could afford to buy a little flat with the work already done. In any other town, maybe, but not this one.

Damn rich people and their damn money.

And damn him for not being one of them.

By lunchtime, Matt was falling asleep at his counter. The shop had been open all morning, although he hadn't expected any customers, but there was no harm in opening while he did a stock take and some admin. Three coffees, a bowl of cereal and some toast later, Matt's aching back slowly lowered him just over his laptop, his eyes closing, darkness taking over.

He lifted his head with a snort when the bell over his shop door tinkled.

'Afternoon, Matthew.'

Matt groaned and checked the time on his phone.

'It is indeed one minute past twelve. Good afternoon, Stanley.'

Stanley, an eighty-year-old retired cartoonist

shuffled into the shop. He carried a cane topped with a silver dragon head that Matt had managed to find for him online, but he didn't use it to walk. It was just there for the vibe, and in case he needed it. Usually, he wore a dark trilby hat and a thick scarf, but only the scarf was on today. Matt glanced out the large shop window.

'Didn't lose your hat, did you, Stanley?' he asked, a little louder than usual on account of Stanley's hearing not being what it was.

'No, no. Didn't take the chance.' Stanley waved him away and moved to the shelves packed with graphic novels. 'Anything new today?'

'Not today, I'm afraid. Next delivery is Thursday.'

Stanley glanced at him.

'That's tomorrow, Matthew.'

'Yup. So it is.'

'I'll come back tomorrow.'

'Okay.' This wasn't a shock. Stanley came in most days, although always at different times, depending on the day and his schedule. 'Looking for anything in particular?'

'Not really,' Stanley admitted. 'My granddaughter's birthday is coming up but apparently she's into something called Kardashi. Have you heard of that?'

Matt smiled.

'The Kardashians?'

'That's the one. You don't sell anything about

that, do you?'

'I'm afraid not, they're not really my cup of tea.'

'Oh, tea.'

Matt slipped off his stool.

'I'll go put the kettle on.'

'Good boy.' Stanley pulled out a graphic novel and shuffled over to an armchair by the window, sitting carefully with a huff and looking out at the wind. 'Dreadful weather today,' he called through the shop.

'Yeah. Is it cold? I haven't been outside yet,' Matt asked, reappearing with a plate of biscuits. Stanley took one and held it, waiting for his tea.

'What about when you came to work?'

'Oh. Yeah. Right. It's, erm, cold and windy, huh?'

Stanley frowned up at Matt.

'Is everything all right, Matthew?'

'Of course. Yeah. It's all good, Stanley. No worries.'

'I feel like there are worries,' Stanley told him, studying his face.

Matt swallowed hard and disappeared to the back to make the tea. He returned with two mugs and set Stanley's down on the small table beside the chair, next to the plate of biscuits. Stanley immediately dunked his biscuit into his tea.

'Tell me what's wrong.'

'Nothing's wrong.'

Stanley raised a hairy, white eyebrow.

'Perhaps I can help.'

A smile tugged at Matt's lips and he crossed his arms, shaking his head.

'I'm fine.'

Stanley stared at him until Matt's smile fell away.

'Fine,' he relented, dropping his arms. 'Lillian said she would leave the flat upstairs to me and she didn't. Which is fine. That's up to her. And I'm so grateful she left me the shop, really I am.'

'But?'

'But I... I don't have anywhere to live right now.' The words spilled out of Matt and he turned away from Stanley, sliding onto his stool behind the counter.

'My boy,' said Stanley slowly, after a short, thoughtful pause. 'You can stay with me.'

Matt's chest tightened.

'That's really good of you, thank you, but I can't impose. I don't want to impose. I'll figure it out.'

'Who did Lillian leave the flat to?' Stanley took a bite of his tea-soaked biscuit.

'I don't know but I think they must have the keys. I heard someone moving around up there last night.'

'You're sleeping here?'

Matt nodded.

'Just for now. Not for long. Please, don't worry. Everything'll be fine.' Matt sighed again without meaning to and looked down at the pile of paperwork underneath his laptop. 'I've been going through everything Lillian and her solicitors have sent me about all this. I must have imagined her telling me she'd leave me the flat. It's wonderful to have the shop, I just need to focus on that.'

'Can you not rent a flat? You can't sleep in your shop over Christmas.'

'It's okay, I'll go to my parents for Christmas,' said Matt absent-mindedly.

'Perhaps Lillian's family would rent the flat to you,' Stanley suggested after some quiet thought.

Matt had considered this. It was something he planned on asking should he bump into whoever now had the keys.

'Maybe. I'm going to ask.'

'No harm in asking,' Stanley agreed, finishing his biscuit and wrapping his fingers around the mug of tea. 'I suppose everything is too expensive otherwise?'

'It is.'

'Damn rich people driving up the prices. Do you know, I've had four people now asking to buy my house.'

Matt wasn't surprised. Stanley had moved to the town before it became a tourist destination and had bought a large, thatched roof cottage with a huge garden on a cartoonist salary. Such a thing just couldn't happen now. He'd then spent the last few decades modernising and extending it. Matt had only visited once, but the house was a thing of beauty, worth a million now, at least. Stanley planned on leaving it to his daughter, who lived in Australia with her family, so she always had a home in the UK.

Matt tried not to think about that too much.

'Will you sell to them?' he asked distractedly.

'Of course not,' said Stanley, sipping his tea. 'Even though they keep offering eye-watering amounts.'

Matt couldn't stop the next sigh even if he tried.

They both sat up, startled, as there came a crash from the back of the shop.

'What was that?' asked Stanley.

'No idea. Hang on.'

Matt made his way to the back of the shop, expecting to find a box fallen to the ground, but there was nothing. Not one thing was out of place. Frowning, Matt returned to the front and Stanley, just as a couple of suited men walked through the door, the bell above them ringing. Matt said hello and left them to browse.

'Nothing fell over, no idea what that was,' he told Stanley.

'Check your back door.'

'I don't have a back door.'

'Oh. Mice?'

Matt glanced at the two customers and lowered his voice.

'Better not be,' he grumbled.

Stanley might not have caught the words, but he got the gist, and grinned. Matt straightened up the solicitor paperwork underneath his laptop, sitting back on his stool, and then looked up as the bell rang again.

The door wasn't open, which was impossible because that was how the bell rang. It was the only way for the bell to ring, unless the wind had somehow made it inside the shop without anyone noticing.

Matt froze. On the other side of the door, key in hand, peering inside, was a familiar face, although he couldn't place her. Heart pounding, he stared at her, forgetting that she could see him just as clearly. She adjusted the bag on her shoulder and offered him a smile. Matt's lips twitched in response although later he wouldn't be able to tell if he managed a smile back.

'Everything okay, Matthew?'

'I don't know,' Matt whispered, staring at the woman, waiting for the spell to break.

6

Despite it being lunchtime, Lilah wasn't hungry. She was still full of coffee and cake enjoyed with Bea. Still, she'd popped into the local supermarket express on her way home and picked up the makings of sandwiches before trudging home against the wind. The shop below her flat was open, which was a shock. There were even people inside. She gazed through the window at the two suited men chatting over something on the shelves, and then at the elderly man sitting in the chair, sipping what she presumed to be tea. She'd been wrong, obviously. It wasn't about whether it was the right season or not, the shop appeared to be something of a community hub. Although one elderly person with a biscuit didn't make a community hub. He might just be a relative or friend of the man behind the counter. The attractive man behind the counter, Lilah corrected herself. He was staring down at his laptop, frowning. His brown hair was almost floppy and he pushed it back out of his eyes.

Lilah didn't move. No one around her moved. The door in front of her didn't move. Yet, the bell above the door, inside the shop, tinkled. She heard it, as did the men inside the shop, and the man behind the counter automatically looked up and locked eyes with her.

Holding her breath, Lilah held his gaze. It was only the bag of paints, bread and cheese slipping from her shoulder that forced her into action. She pulled the bag back up her shoulder and attempted a smile. Whether this man owned the shop or just worked there, she needed to make a good impression, given that she'd be living just upstairs.

When the man didn't move – no one moved – Lilah cleared her throat, shivered as a gust of wind found her, and went to unlock her front door. Instead of putting the key in the lock, however, she found herself pushing open the door to the shop, the bell ringing out again.

Lilah stepped inside, the door closing on the weather behind her, and she stood for a moment, her eyes still on the man behind the counter. She flashed him another quick smile and turned away, into the shop.

'Hi,' he said as she turned. 'Let me know if I can help you with anything.'

It was obviously what he said to all new customers, so she nodded, thanking him silently. The shop was lined with shelves, and there was a table in the middle full of things to buy. The shelves were packed. The one she was now facing held books, bigger than Lilah was used to and many of them much thinner than she expected. A couple were positioned to show their covers, full of bright colours and superheroes. The next shelves over held boxes of board games she was vaguely familiar with and some she'd never heard of. Over on the other side of the shop were glass cabinets of action figures. On one wall were swords that couldn't possibly be real. Lilah turned slowly, taking it all in.

She'd known it was essentially a comic book shop from the outside, of course. A shop full of fantasy and science fiction, of superheroes and other worlds, but it had been such a long time since she'd set foot in one it came as quite a shock. She didn't know what to look at first and settled on a whole bookcase of boxed stylised figures with the names of the characters they represented written below them.

When she'd last visited Lillian, back when she was a teenager, this shop had still been the book-shop that Lillian had run. Lilah had even worked in it one summer.

The shape and layout of the shop hadn't changed much, just the stock.

She went back to the graphic novels and read some of the titles, but nothing called out to her. Knowing how much Lillian had supported this shop, Lilah wanted to support them too. She wanted to continue Lillian's legacy as much as possible, and that meant buying something. The problem was she wasn't much of a fan of these things. There was no room in the flat for action figures or collectibles, and she had no use for them. Books were great, but Lilah had never gotten on with graphic novels. There were t-shirts, and Lilah looked through them, considering buying something oversized to wear in the evenings before bed, or on lazy, rainy days.

There were quite a few t-shirts she didn't understand, so she ignored those. One t-shirt had an illustrated cartoon goat standing proud beneath a rainbow with 'I am the GOAT' written around it. It was in her size, the goat was cute, she understood the reference and discovered she was smiling. Picking up the t-shirt, she headed to the counter.

'Hi,' she murmured as the man looked up, his brown eyes wide.

'Hi.' He took the t-shirt from her and scanned it.

'Erm, I'm living in the flat upstairs,' she started, desperately trying to work out if he was the owner or an employee. 'Is this your shop?' she asked meekly.

'Yeah. I'm Matt.' He looked away, finding a bag for her.

'Oh, don't worry about the bag, I'm just going upstairs.' Lilah laughed, her voice breaking a little, and she snapped her mouth shut. 'So, you knew my Aunt Lillian?'

Matt stopped and looked up at her slowly.

'Lilly was your aunt,' he murmured. 'Yeah, yeah, I knew her.'

'And she left you her shop.' Lilah grinned, looking around. 'I love it.'

Visibly relaxing, Matt smiled, also looking around, his gaze landing on the two men who were whispering over the collectibles.

'Yeah. It was really good of her.'

'What's that?' shouted the elderly man behind Lilah.

She jumped and turned to look at him, plastering on a smile.

'She lives upstairs. Lillian is – was – her aunt,' Matt almost shouted. 'Sorry,' he murmured, his cheeks turning a pleasing shade of pink. 'Stanley's a little hard of hearing.'

Lilah stared at him, watching him fluster, her own nerves calming. Still, there was something about him.

'Lilah,' she said. 'I'm Lilah,' she shouted back to the man in the chair. 'Lillian's niece.'

'Ah! I'm Stanley, a pleasure to meet Lillian's niece,' said Stanley, holding out a hand.

Lilah took it and shook. Stanley's hand was warm and he squeezed gently, although his gaze flittered back to Matt and he raised a questioning eyebrow. Lilah turned back to Matt, confused.

'Twenty pounds, please,' said Matt.

'Oh, right. Yes.' Lilah took out her phone and waved it over Matt's card machine until it beeped.

He handed her the t-shirt along with a receipt.

'How long have you been here?' she asked. 'With the shop, I mean.'

'About five years.'

Lilah nodded, leaving too long a gap as she searched for something else to say. The silence stretched before them.

'It's a nice flat, I believe,' said Stanley, behind her.

'Oh, yes. Yes, it is,' Lilah agreed. 'I'm still going through a lot of her stuff.'

There was another silence as Stanley looked at Matt and Matt stared down at his laptop. Lilah pressed her lips together, studying him but not wanting to make him uncomfortable. That was when it hit her.

'Were you at Lillian's funeral?'

Matt glanced up quickly and then looked away.

'Er, yeah, I was.'

'We talked, didn't we? Over the cake? The disgusting carrot cake that she would have hated.'

'Yeah, yeah, I think so.'

Lilah grinned.

'How weird! If only we'd known then that we'd be neighbours, huh?'

'Ha. Yeah.'

Another silence stretched out, Lilah's grin frozen in place as she waited for something else to happen. The two men in suits left the shop, the bell ringing out their departure.

'Okay, well, it was nice to meet you,' said Lilah. 'Nice to meet both of you. I guess I'll probably see you again.' She looked at Matt until he met her gaze and this time he didn't look away.

'Sure. Yeah, nice to meet you too. Lilah.'

'Okay.' Lilah held the t-shirt to her chest and turned away, smiling at Stanley. She walked through the shop's door, listening to the bell ringing overhead, and then found her door key. Only once she was through her front door did her grin fall and she stopped.

Was it her or had that whole encounter been strange? Perhaps Matt was just shy. It was very Lillian to want to help a young person who wasn't good at talking to people start a business.

Lilah made her way up the stairs. All in all, the day had been a success and very full. She'd met three new people and that was quite enough. Once in her flat, she put the paints and art supplies away, along with the food she'd bought, and then disappeared into the bedroom, throwing her new t-shirt on the bed. Slipping into the bathroom, she put the shower on and undressed as the water warmed. She'd have a hot shower, then a cup of tea and read a book. It was time to relax.

She stepped under the hot water, smiling again, marking the first day of her new life a success. The shop owner downstairs was not only attractive, he was the Gorgeous Funeral Man. Wait until her mother heard! Lilah had mentioned him but no one in the family had been able to place him. So many of Lillian's friends had turned up and the family hadn't known most of them. Still, Matt was her neighbour, so she didn't want to do anything that might upset them working and living side by side.

She would pop into the shop another time, buy something and try again to talk. He was obviously open to friendship if Lillian had liked him enough to leave him her shop, and if Stanley was comfortable enough to sit in a chair, read a graphic novel and drink tea. Maybe Matt only liked talking to older people.

She laughed to herself as the hot water ran through her windswept hair, washing away the saltwater spray. Maybe Matt would come around once he realised she only wanted to support him, as Lillian had.

7

'I can't believe I ever wanted to ask her out. At a funeral! It must have been the grief.' Matt followed Danny along the edge of the football pitch as a bunch of teenagers ran around in front of them. If Matt paid more attention, he would see the formations Danny had given the players, rather than a bunch of teenagers milling about.

'But she's pretty, yeah?' said Danny, breathlessly. 'Oi! Nicholls, stay open!'

'Well, yeah.'

'So that's why you wanted to ask her out.' Danny quickly sidestepped the other way and Matt turned around and followed, his brow creased in thought.

'I should have known, though. Of course she's Lillian's niece.'

'Why of course? Brown! Hobbs! Attack! Get the ball!'

'She has a look about her,' Matt murmured without much confidence. 'I don't know. It doesn't matter now, does it? She's the enemy.'

Danny stopped and looked at his friend with a sigh. Matt met his gaze and then jumped as Danny blew his whistle so hard Matt was pretty sure his hair moved in the wind the whistle created.

'She's not the enemy, you're being ridiculous,' Danny told him before turning and marching onto the pitch. 'Who can tell me what went wrong there? How did the ball get through that defence?'

Matt didn't hear the students' responses. He crossed his arms and remained at the edge of the pitch, staring down at the muddy grass. The wind had dropped, thankfully, and the forecasted rain had held off long enough that Danny's football coaching of the local youth team could happen outside. Matt wasn't sure if that was a good thing or not. He assumed, given the amount of mud on the teenagers', that their parents would say it wasn't.

Danny kicked the ball to a boy and then turned and wandered back to Matt, blowing his whistle and restarting the game.

'She has my flat, is all I mean,' said Matt.

'She's your new neighbour, not your enemy,' Danny told him, watching the game. 'And hey, your new neighbour is pretty and you want to ask her out. So.'

Matt looked up at him.

'So?'

'So, ask her out. Idiot,' Danny muttered.

Matt frowned.

'Who's the idiot? Me?'

Danny laughed, looking at his friend.

'Did you hear me blow the whistle? Yes, mate, you. You're the idiot.'

'Well, what do you want me to do? What do I do? Tell me.'

'I've already told you, Matty. Move in with your parents for the time being and ask this woman out on a date. Things will get better. They always do.' Danny put his whistle to his mouth and this time Matt had the forethought to brace himself.

The footballers stopped and one shouted to Danny, pointing at another boy.

'I don't want to hear it!' Danny shouted back, marching into the fray.

Matt stared off towards the horizon, to the other side of the town's football pitch where there was a fence, places for families to stand, and beyond that, trees and allotments. Danny returned, blowing his whistle again, the ball shooting past them followed by two boys.

'I don't want to move in with my parents,' said Matt. 'And who wants to date the failure downstairs who lives with his parents?'

'She'll understand. It's tough out there right now. Maybe she'll offer you the second bedroom. Or hers.' Danny elbowed Matt playfully and Matt smiled, as if he hadn't considered that during the hours after Lilah had left his shop, his stomach in knots.

'I could move in with your parents,' Matt

suggested, flashing Danny a grin as Danny shot him a look.

'Your parents are nice people, Matt.'

'I know, of course they are. They raised me! Look how great I am. This is just a stumbling block, I know.' A really big stumbling block that had been dragging on for too long now. Matt loved his parents with all his heart, and he knew they loved him, but he couldn't stand one more conversation about how he should be making better money by now. Like he didn't know. Like that would help his housing situation.

'Have you been checking the property listings?' Danny asked before sidestepping away from Matt, following the ball as it moved up the pitch.

'Yeah. Yeah, nothing came on today.'

'And the estate agents all know you exist?'

'Yup.'

'Something will come up. Yes!' Danny threw his arms up and then caught himself, clearing his throat, as the ball hit the back of the net. He blew his whistle before anyone could say anything and ran onto the pitch, no doubt to teach his students another valuable lesson about teamwork.

Matt watched him, wondering not for the first time what he could have done differently. What other path he could have taken. If he'd joined Danny on his teaching course, would he be assistant football coach with a wife and small child at home? Still living in Danny's shadow, but fine with that. He'd always been fine living in Danny's shadow. There was something about the quiet ambition in Danny that Matt had always found awe-inspiring but also impossible to match.

There would come a point where Matt could concede that he should explain his housing situation to his parents and ask for his old childhood bedroom back temporarily. It wasn't like he couldn't afford to pay bills, he would pay his share and help around the house as much as they'd let him. It was the taste of it all that he couldn't stomach at that moment. An affordable flat would come up and he'd get it. He just had to be patient.

In the meantime, he had no choice but to carry on working hard, building up his business and his savings, and...

'You think I should ask her out?'

Danny came back to the edge of the pitch, blowing his whistle. The teenagers had arranged themselves to take penalties and Danny leaned forward, hands on his knees, to watch.

'Yes.'

'If she says no, I'll never be able to look my new neighbour in the eye again.'

'Then don't.'

Matt blew out his cheeks.

'I couldn't even get my words out when she came in the shop, Dan. I was a mess.'

'Then ask her.'

'And then she'll find out I'm sleeping in the

shop.'

'Parents.'

'Is that better than sleeping in the shop?'

Danny gave Matt a sideways look and straighten-ed. Patting his friend on the shoulder, he looked Matt in the eye and said, 'I don't know, mate. Do what you want to.'

Then he marched back onto the pitch, blowing his whistle and shouting to the goalkeeper as one boy kicked the ball into the goal.

Matt watched him blindly, wondering what type of flowers one bought for the woman who inadvert-ently stole a flat from you.

8

It was the day after Lilah had met Matt and despite having spent the morning by the beach, with Bea, painting and learning and ruining another page in her sketchbook, she hadn't been able to get Matt out of her head. Was he shy? Is that why he'd fumbled his words so much when she'd gone into the shop? It had been closed when she'd gone out that morning, but open when she returned, although Matt couldn't be seen from the door.

She was sorting through more of Lillian's things, mostly clothes, holding some up against herself at the mirror before deciding whether to keep or donate it. She would visit Matt's shop again but perhaps not today. Two days in a row was probably excessive.

Lilah jumped when a ringing sounded through the flat and she stopped, trying to work out what it was. It couldn't be the smoke alarm, that beeped. And it hadn't been her phone, behind her on the bed, although that was where she looked first. Was it coming from outside?

After a while, it sounded again.

'Oh. Doorbell.' Lilah dropped the clothes she was holding and rushed through the flat, down the stairs to the front door. She opened it without thinking, realising her mistake as she did so, and then froze.

Matt looked up with wide eyes as the door opened, his body twisted as if he'd been in the process of leaving. Lilah's stomach flipped and she held on to the door to stay upright.

'Hi,' she breathed.

He was dressed in jeans and a black hoody, as he had been the day before in the shop. In fact, she was pretty sure they were the same jeans and hoody. His hair was ruffled, although not from the wind which had now died down. It was likely from him running his hand through it.

'Hi. Erm, just wanted to welcome you. I know I was a bit off yesterday. You caught me by surprise. Erm, here. Welcome.' He handed her a small bouquet of flowers that he'd been holding behind his back and gave a small shrug as if frustrated.

Lilah smiled.

'That's so sweet. Thank you.'

They were yellow roses. Lilah took the flowers and looked up into Matt's eyes. He was taller than her, around six foot, although he stooped a little. He met her gaze and held it for a moment.

'Do you want to come in?' Lilah found herself

asking.

Matt blinked and glanced into his shop. 'I understand if you can't,' Lilah added quickly. 'It's just you were obviously close to Lillian. Right? Yellow roses,' she said quietly, holding the flowers to her face although there wasn't a scent. 'She loved yellow.'

'Force of habit, I guess,' said Matt, frowning at the flowers. 'I was always safe with yellow.'

Lilah gave a small laugh and stepped aside.

'You're very welcome to come in.' If Lillian trusted Matt, enough to leave him her shop, then Lilah trusted him too.

Matt bit his lip and nodded once, stepping inside. He closed the door behind him as Lilah led the way up the stairs. She went straight to the kitchen, finding a vase and filling it with water. Matt followed slowly, looking around as he went.

'How long did you know Lillian?' Lilah asked as she cut the bottom off each stem and arranged them in the vase.

'About seven years, I guess,' said Matt, standing in the doorway. 'I've had the shop for five years. She was always so kind about it. Never put the rent up.'

'She was always so kind,' Lilah agreed. 'I was surprised you were open. I guessed that most shops here were seasonal. It's so quiet here right now. Do you get many Christmas shoppers?'

'Mostly locals,' said Matt. 'It's busier in the summer. The whole town is. But I couldn't survive without the locals and being open all year round.'

'Of course,' Lilah murmured, hoping she hadn't said anything wrong. 'What made you start your own business?' She flashed him a smile. 'I'm hoping to start my own. It's one of the reasons I'm here.'

They stared at one another for a moment, Lilah waiting for Matt to decide whether to answer.

'Would you like a cup of tea?' she asked when he didn't respond.

'Sure.'

'Milk? Sugar?'

'Milk, no sugar. Please. Thanks.'

Lilah filled the kettle and Matt leaned against the door frame, his arms crossed against his chest. She spotted his stance from the corner of her eye and did her best to ignore it, no matter how much she wanted to look at him properly.

'I've always wanted my own comic book shop,' he said eventually. 'Always wanted to be my own boss. I got the opportunity, so I took it.'

He was holding back. Lilah nodded, plastering on a smile as she clicked the kettle into action.

'Same here. Guess you have to take the opportunity when you get it. I was made redundant and haven't had much luck in finding a new job.'

There was a long silence and Lilah tried to think of something else to ask him, her mind blank with growing panic.

'What business do you want to start?' he asked quietly.

'I want to be an artist,' she said carefully and quietly, not quite trusting the words. She glanced at him sideways.

'What kind of artist?' he asked, as if it was the most normal question, which she supposed it was.

'Paints, I think. I'm not sure. I'd like to try lots of things, but I was good at drawing and painting when I was younger. I loved it, always thought that's what I'd do. I used to dream of living by the coast and painting the sea every day.' The kettle finished boiling and Lilah occupied herself making the tea. 'Then life got in the way and I had to get an office job.'

'Yeah, I hate those.'

Lilah grinned as she passed Matt his cup.

'Yeah? What did you use to do?'

'Graphic design.'

'Oh. I did that, too. Then I got forced into digital marketing, then made redundant.'

Matt gave her a sympathetic look and she laughed. His eyes lightened, the tension shifting.

'Come sit down,' she offered, showing him into the living room, just off the kitchen, and taking the vase of yellow roses with her. She put them on the windowsill, knowing that's where Lillian had always kept freshly cut flowers.

'I'm glad Lillian left you the shop,' she murmured, gazing at the roses. 'It's such a thing she would do. Making sure she looked after everyone.'

'Hmm.' Matt sat on the edge of the sofa, sipping

his tea.

Wrapping her fingers around her cup, Lilah glanced back to him.

'It must be a relief, knowing you own it? I hope there aren't extra costs or anything that come with it? I don't know much about property ownership.'

'No. Me neither. So, she left you this flat?' Matt asked, looking up at her.

'Yes. I don't know how she knew but somehow she always did.'

'Knew what?'

'What I needed.' Lilah sat on the other end of the sofa, sipping her drink, hoping the scalding heat would take the stabbing pain of grief away as it surfaced.

'Right.'

She looked at him properly this time. What had changed? For a moment there, he'd relaxed, perhaps even let the real him slip through. Lilah had liked it, she wanted more of it. Then he'd closed himself off again. She studied him, trying to work it out.

'Didn't she do that with you? Leaving you the shop because she knew you needed it. So you don't have to worry about us putting the rent up or anything.'

'Or anything,' Matt mumbled. 'Yeah, no, I'm grateful. Of course. Don't think I'd ever get to own property if it wasn't for Lillian. Of course I appreciate it. It's just...'

'What?'

'No. Never mind. It doesn't matter.' Matt looked around the living room, up at the walls and ceiling. 'It's nice to have someone upstairs again. It got too quiet for a while there. Nice to know I'm not alone,' he added quietly.

Lilah barely heard him.

'It's just what?'

He met her gaze and visibly swallowed.

'Nothing. It's fine.'

'Okay. But if there's anything... If there's a problem... I want to know about it.'

Matt sighed and put his half-drunk cup of tea down on the coffee table near the sofa.

'Okay. It's just that I knew Lillian was leaving me the shop.'

'Okay.'

'And I thought it came with the flat. I must have misunderstood and that's my fault.'

Lilah's stomach dropped and she put her cup of tea on the table.

'Oh. I had no idea. Did Lillian tell you she'd leave you the flat?'

'I thought she did. But maybe she didn't.'

'She was on a lot of medication towards the end.'

'Yeah. It doesn't matter. It's done now, and I'm lucky to have the shop.'

'Yeah,' Lilah echoed. 'That's why you were off with me? You're annoyed I got the flat?'

Matt shuffled in his seat.

'Just annoying when Londoners come here thinking they own the place when people who grew up here can't afford to stay in their own hometown,' he grumbled.

Lilah's world stopped, if only for a moment, and then a ball of rage dropped into her belly, constricting her throat as she fought to stay calm.

'I'm not from London,' she said carefully, unclenching her teeth.

'Okay.'

'My mum grew up here, in this town, with Lillian. They were born and raised here.'

'Yeah. I know, Lillian was from here.' Matt met her eyes. 'But you aren't. That's all I mean. But it's okay. It makes sense. Lillian didn't have children to leave this place to, so of course she left it to family who don't live here anymore. Like Stanley—'

'So you thought she should leave it to you instead?'

'—No, no, that's not what—'

'Did you see her at the end?'

'What?'

'At the end. Before she died. Were you there?'

'Well, no.'

'No. Do you know why?'

Matt sighed deeply and ran a hand through his hair. Lilah ignored it. Now wasn't the time.

'Because I'm not family?' Matt stood. 'Look, I'm sorry. I didn't mean to upset you. I came in peace. It's just a bad time, and—'

'Because you didn't get the flat? Like now isn't a bad time for me? I've lost my job, my aunt, and left everything I know behind to start again in this flat full of memories. You think that isn't a bad time? You weren't there with her because you're not family. But I was there. She moved in with my parents during her last weeks. Did you know that? And I was living there too because I'd lost my job and I had nothing.'

Matt flinched, something moving across his expression, but the red mist had descended over Lilah and she couldn't stop now.

'I was with her at the end. Those last few weeks. I spent every day with her, seeing how much pain she was in. Do you know what? She never mentioned you. Not once. She didn't tell me she was leaving me the flat. I didn't find out about this or you and your shop until after she passed. So don't come up here giving me all this rubbish about her making you promises.'

'I didn't—'

'I think you should go.'

'Yeah. I think so, too,' Matt murmured, turning to leave.

Lilah watched him, pressing her lips together to stop anything else falling out, her mind a mess of jumbled words still unsaid. Hot tears pricked at her eyes as Matt made his way down the stairs and she started to follow. A part of her wanted to call out, to stop him, but she didn't. She didn't say a word, despite the apology already forming on her tongue.

'Sorry,' Matt said before opening the front door and closing it behind him. He didn't even slam it.

Tears fell down Lilah's cheeks and she growled out a huff, slamming the door at the top of the stairs shut and feeling the building tremble a little around her. She had to go lock the front door, but she couldn't bear the thought of the stairs at that moment. Instead, she rushed into her bedroom and threw herself on her bed, curling into a ball and letting the sobs take over, her tears staining her duvet cover.

As she cried, the door at the top of the stairs somehow opened, although no one was on the other side. The curtains in Lilah's bedroom fluttered a little and she closed her eyes, not feeling as cold as she thought she would.

'I'm sorry,' she said into the duvet, thinking of the yellow roses in the window and the scent of Lillian that still filled the flat. 'I miss you so much.'

9

The shop was empty all afternoon, so Matt sat at the counter and went through everything he'd received from the solicitors and Lillian again. He knew it all by heart now, but still, he must have missed something. Surely.

Lilah's words repeated at the back of his head, burning themselves into his mind. He knew he'd overstepped. He should have just been grateful for the shop and left it at that. Why hadn't he been able to just leave it? To say hi to Lilah when she first appeared in his shop, been polite, but otherwise ignored her? What was wrong with him?

Swallowing hard, Matt stared down at the solicitor's paperwork he'd so carefully printed out, just in case it all turned out to be a dream. He wanted nothing more in that moment than to set fire to it all.

A loud crash sounded from the back of the shop and Matt jumped, his head snapping up. Heart pounding from the fright, he sighed and made his way over to the sound, where something must have fallen over.

As he reached the back shelves, hidden away from the rest of the shop, he saw the outline of a woman looking at some figurines and managed to stop himself from squealing in shock. Matt cleared his throat, glanced back to the front of the shop, wondering how she'd managed to sneak in without him noticing, and turned back to say hello.

She was gone.

Frantic, Matt looked around him and then began searching the shop. There wasn't much to search so it didn't take long. Frowning, ignoring his stomach turning over, Matt searched again, meticulously this time. He even checked inside the boxes in the back room.

Finally, he stood in the middle of the shop and said, 'Hello?'

No one answered. The bell hadn't rung to announce the door opening. By now, enough time had passed that he decided he must have imagined the whole thing. Rubbing a hand down his face, he returned to the back of the shop and made himself a cup of strong coffee. Then he walked slowly to the counter and went back to thinking.

The first thing he needed to do was apologise to Lilah. If they were going to be neighbours, then they needed to get on. He'd gone into her home and upset her, so he needed to apologise. Yellow roses wouldn't work this time.

He looked down at the paperwork, ready to scoop it up and put it away, when he spotted an envelope that hadn't been there before. It was small, white and sealed, with his name written in curly handwriting on the front. Matt blinked. How had he not noticed this before? Had someone walked in while he was in the back and left it there? The bell hadn't rung once, and the envelope was beneath three pieces of paper, as if it had always been there, unnoticed.

Except that Matt had gone through everything multiple times. How had he missed it?

Chewing on his lip, he opened the envelope and pulled out a small, folded letter.

Dearest Matt,

My friend.
You must be wondering why I didn't leave you my flat. There are not enough apologies in the world. I'm going back on my promise to you, but I must explain that it is for a good reason.

Ha! Matt fell back onto his stool and reread that beginning three times. Here it was. Proof that he hadn't made it up, he hadn't imagined Lillian's promise. She acknowledged it. Pausing, he quickly checked the name at the end of the letter. Yes, it was from Lillian. And here was the promise in writing.

In the end, I had to leave the flat to my niece. It was always hers, I just didn't see it. But then, I think it was always yours too.
Please know that life has not been particularly kind to her of late, which is why I must go back on my promise to you.

I hope the shop is enough to keep you safe and content. Please do sell it if you need to. You are never beholden to it.

Matt, promise me something. Even though I couldn't keep my promise to you.
Promise that you will be kind to yourself, allow yourself happiness, stop saying the word 'should' and talk to my niece when she moves in.
I think you'll like her.

Sending you love and coffee from the Other Side.

Lillian

The letter was signed with little hand-drawn hearts and kisses. Matt read the letter again and took a gulp of his coffee.

'Damn it,' he mumbled.

How had he missed this? Putting the letter back in the envelope and over to one side, he went through everything else, trying to work it out. What else had he missed?

There, another envelope with a solicitor letter folded in half inside and here was a paperclip. Lillian's envelope must have been hidden inside the letter, the only correspondence sent to him through the post. That was how he'd missed it. Then how had it come to be near the top of the pile without the paperclip?

Matt sighed again and drained his coffee, his chest tightening a little. He stood and stretched and groaned into the empty shop, and then, when another crash sounded at the back, screamed, 'Why?' at the top of his voice.

This time he rushed across the shop, searching every corner. While there were no figures of women that shouldn't be there, he could have sworn he saw a shadow moving where ordinarily there wouldn't be a shadow, and then, down on the carpeted floor were yellow petals.

Slowly, carefully, holding his breath, Matt approached them and bent to retrieve the petals. They were soft and seemed to be from roses. He looked up at the ceiling, as if they'd magically fallen through Lilah's floor into his shop. Matt shook his head, gathered the petals and returned to the counter. Someone had walked them in and he hadn't noticed.

That was all.

He put the petals in the bin and pulled out his phone.

Mate. You free? Weird stuff happening here today and just found a letter from Lillian.

He sent the message to Danny and left the phone on the counter while he tidied away the solicitor paperwork, putting it in a folder and then the folder in the safe under the counter. He left the letter from Lillian by his phone. What he needed right then was a home where he could keep important things, instead of a safe and a sleeping bag in his shop.

Lilah's words came back to him. She'd gone back to her parents when she'd run out of choices, maybe he just had to accept that he needed to call his parents and ask them to take pity on him.

His phone buzzed against the wooden counter and Matt took the welcome distraction.

I'm down the park. You're welcome to join us. What weird stuff? What does the letter say?

Matt didn't need to be told twice. He grabbed Lillian's letter and his keys, went into the back to grab his coat and a woolly hat that he rammed on his head over his ears, then he locked the shop behind him and jogged down the road.

It didn't take long to get to the park near Danny's house. He found Danny sitting on a bench inside the fenced-off play area, watching his four-year-old looking up at the climbing frame.

'Why's she just looking at it?' Matt asked breathlessly, collapsing onto the bench next to Danny.

'She's got an idea in her head and she's planning it out.'

'Uh oh.'

'Yeah, uh oh. I've already told her it's not a good idea, but you try convincing her otherwise.' Danny looked up at Matt and studied him. 'Actually, that's a good idea. You go convince her otherwise. She might listen to Uncle Matty.'

Matt grinned and gave Lillian's letter to Danny, smacking him on the chest with it.

'Sure. Found this. No idea why I didn't see it before. Also, things keep falling down in my shop and making a crashing noise but when I look, nothing's actually moved. Saw a woman who wasn't there. Found yellow rose petals on the floor where there hadn't been any before.' Matt smacked his thighs and stood up, wandering over to Danny's daughter. 'Hey, Rosie.'

Rosie, her braided hair in pigtails, looked up at Matt and beamed, her eyes brightening.

'Matty!'

'Your dad tells me you're planning something?' Matt crouched beside Rosie and looked up at the climbing frame, trying to ignore how daunting it was from this low down. 'What's the plan?'

'Gonna climb to the top and hang upside down by my legs,' Rosie told him proudly.

Matt's heart skipped a beat.

'Yeah? That sounds... scary.'

'Nah. I can do it.'

'Oh, I have no doubt about that. You're strong and clever, but you know, you'll scare the life out of me and your dad.'

'You don't have to be scared.'

'But we will be anyway. Much better to not do that, don't you think? Because you know you can, and that's the important part. Right? How about we go on the swings? I'll push you.'

Rosie looked over at the swings and then up to the top of the climbing frame, her lips pursed in deep thought.

'But I wanna do it.'

'It's too windy to go that high, Rosie.' Matt watched the child, his mind racing. 'And cold. Brr. Don't you feel that? Hey, don't tell your dad I told you this, but did you know that if you lick something metal when it's really cold and icy, like the swing frame over there, your tongue sticks to it?'

Rosie's eyes widened as Matt spoke and then she twirled around and ran fast back to Danny sitting on the bench, reading Lillian's letter.

'Daddy!'

'Yes, pumpkin?' Danny quickly put the letter to the side and caught Rosie as she threw herself at him. 'Matty says that if you lick the swing frame, your tongue sticks to it.'

Danny pulled a face and looked up at Matt as he approached. Rosie was pulled properly onto Danny's lap before he passed the letter back to

Matt.

'Shh!' Matty feigned an angry look at Rosie. 'And you missed out the ice. It has to be icy.'

Rosie nodded.

'Daddy! If you lick the swing frame when it's icy, your tongue sticks to it!'

'That's how you stop her climbing frame plan?' Danny mumbled, holding his daughter close.

Matt shrugged.

'Worked, didn't it? And it's not icy. Don't worry.'

Danny huffed and pulled Rosie up so she could look him in the eye. He waited until he had her attention.

'Rosie. Do not lick the swing frame. Okay? That's disgusting.'

Rosie was already distracted.

'When does the ice come?' she asked Matt.

Danny shot him a look.

'Nah, you don't want to do that,' Matt told her. 'Boys leave their bogies on the swing frame.'

'Ew!' Rosie screamed, clapping a hand over her mouth.

'Ew,' said Danny.

Matt laughed at them both. Danny pressed his lips to Rosie's head, kissing her hard and loud.

'You can climb halfway up the climbing frame and no further,' he told her. 'I'm watching.'

Rosie kissed him back and leapt off his lap, running full speed to the climbing frame.

'Mate, I get her away from it and you send her

right back.'

Danny turned to Matt, keeping an eye on his daughter.

'What're you going to do now?' he asked, gesturing at the enveloped letter in Matt's hand.

'I don't know,' Matt murmured, sliding the letter into his coat. 'Apologise. Properly.'

'And?'

Matt looked up into Danny's eyes and pressed his lips together.

'And nothing. That's all there is, isn't there. Lillian wanted her niece to have the flat and me to have the shop. I'm incredibly lucky.'

'Call your parents?' Danny suggested, lifting off the bench as Rosie climbed higher.

'Yeah. Yeah, maybe.' Matt followed, ambling along behind, his gaze on the ground. 'I'll figure it out. What about the bangs in the shop?'

'The what?'

'It sounds like something's falling over but nothing has fallen over. And there was a woman. I saw her. And then she was gone.' He frowned. 'Do you think—'

'I think you're stressed, Matt. You need proper sleep that doesn't come from sleeping on your shop floor.'

'Technically it's the floor of the back room.'

'Same thing,' said Danny, reaching up and tapping his daughter's arm. She turned and looked down at him, scowled and climbed down a rung.

'Maybe get a hotel room for the night or something, get some proper sleep?'

'In a hotel room? Where thousands have slept before me? No, thanks.'

'I'd invite you to stay at ours, but I know it won't go down well.'

'Nah, you're okay. Thank you, I appreciate it, but if Nat's waters break while I'm there, I'll just be another person panicking.'

'You'll be the only person panicking. We've been through it before.' Danny pointed to Rosie just above him, now climbing sideways, and he stepped along so he was always under her.

'Yeah, and you don't want that.'

'Nope. So, call your parents?'

Matt sighed, looking up at the grey sky.

'Hey, Rosie, excited for Santa coming to visit?'

Danny glowered at his friend as Rosie screamed and began to hurriedly climb down, shouting about Christmas coming at the top of her voice.

10

Sitting on the sofa in the living room, Lilah was desperately trying to concentrate on where the Christmas tree should go, but all her mind would offer was Matt's words on repeat. Lillian had promised him the flat.

She knew it didn't matter. She had the title deeds, now in her name. She had the keys and the solicitor's paperwork. This flat was hers.

Anyway, what would Matt have done with all of Lillian's stuff? Lilah looked around at the furniture, photos in their frames and ornaments. They would have had to clear it out before he was handed the whole thing. She was glad Lillian hadn't left it to him. The agony of clearing out her aunt's home for someone she'd never met would have eaten her up inside. It had been a relief to know that they could go through everything at their own pace, or rather at Lilah's pace as she settled in.

Her mother had suggested she move in after Christmas, but Lilah had wanted to air the flat, to do something other than nothing every day, to see the ocean at Christmas. Was the front lit up? Did the lights twinkle on the waves when the tide was in? These were questions Lilah needed the answer to this year, not next.

She wanted to start her new life, and she could hardly do that if the man in the shop below thought he should own her new home.

Lilah sighed and leaned across the sofa to her laptop, resting on the sofa cushion. Pulling it onto her lap, she opened it, unlocked it and went straight to the folder she'd been using the most of late: the folder labelled 'FLAT'. Inside were all of the files her solicitor had sent her.

She went through each file, ignoring the statement of what was included with the flat, who owned the utilities, where the flat's boundaries ended and the shop's began, until she found a file about the separation of the flat and shop. Lillian had gotten the deeds legally separated before she passed, just as she'd organised most things before her death, including almost every detail of her own funeral. Apart from the dress code, and the presence of carrot cake, it turned out.

Halfway through the legal talk, her brain already hurting, Lilah shoved the laptop aside and went to put the kettle on. She returned with a cup of coffee, pulled the laptop back to her and continued reading. She didn't stop until she'd gone through every piece of official paperwork and every email the solicitor had sent her.

In every piece of correspondence, the flat was hers.

She went back further, to the letters and emails from Lillian's solicitor, and checked everything again.

There was no mention of Matt, other than to say that the flat and the shop were being separated and Lillian was leaving the flat, mortgage free, to Lilah.

Having finished her coffee, Lilah stood and stretched her back, glancing out the window. She wondered briefly what the sea was doing at that moment and was tempted to grab her coat and go find out.

Glancing back to her laptop on the sofa, she made a quick decision. Sitting, she opened a new email and typed out her thoughts, rereading it a few times and editing as she went to make it more formal. Then she hit send and went to grab her coat. As she began to pull it on, her phone started to ring, buzzing against her leg in her pocket. Dropping her coat, Lilah checked her phone and smiled, abandoning plans to go out for a moment. She climbed back up the stairs, dropped back onto the sofa and answered the phone.

'Hi, Mum.'

'Merry December! How's it going there? Are you lonely? Are you bored? Do you want to come home for Christmas now?'

Lilah laughed.

'Sorry, but it's actually so lovely here.'

'Oh good! You're not lonely?'

'Not really. I haven't had a chance.' Lilah looked around the room, smiling. 'Remember Lillian's friend I told you about? Bea?'

'Yes.'

'Well, I went out with her again yesterday. We meet, we paint, we go for coffee and cake.'

'That sounds like bliss. And you're painting the ocean?'

'Yep, and every day it's different. I mean, the sky is always grey right now, but some days the waves are big and sometimes they're small, some days it's angry and other days, not so much. Some days there's blue on the water for no apparent reason, but mostly it's grey.'

'Should I send you money for more grey paint?'

'Shockingly, Lillian had a lot of the stuff.'

Her mother laughed.

'How are you?' Lilah asked.

'Coping,' said her mother in a softer tone. 'But the house is too quiet. First Lillian is gone and now you.'

'It's not quite the same.'

'No, of course not. But the silence sort of is.'

Lilah bit her lip as her chest tightened.

'I'm sorry. I guess I didn't really think that through. I can come home if you want?' Lilah didn't want to, but the grief wouldn't stay this fresh forever and maybe she had left home too abruptly.

'No, no. It's fine. You should be out there, living your life. It's what I want for you, and I know it's what Lillian wanted. She wanted that flat lived in and loved.'

'Yeah, but I can come home now until after Christmas. It's only a few weeks.'

'No. We stick to the plan. I'm okay. Really. Your dad is looking after me. We're fine. Have you spoken to Emily recently?'

'I messaged her the day I moved in,' Lilah told her mother. 'Sent her a video of the sea.'

'That's lovely.'

'Yeah, she sent me a photo back of the mountains, as if Italian mountains beat the British coast in December.'

Her mother laughed and Lilah grinned, glad to have brought the mood up. 'She mentioned she's staying in Italy for Christmas?' she added quietly.

'It's not our turn this year. But next year! And me and your dad have been talking about going to Italy in the summer, or spring, before it gets too hot. You're welcome to join us?'

'Yeah, that sounds nice. I might do that,' Lilah said gently, picturing her sister's face and the days they'd spend lounging around her sister's pool with her children, eating ice cream. It sounded heavenly and Lilah was distracted for a moment by the thought of painting the mountains in the photo Emily had sent her. Sitting by the pool, paintbrush in hand, and beside her...

There was a pause as Lilah considered how to word her next question.

'Mum. Did Lillian ever mention a Matt to you?'

'Amatt? What's an amatt?'

'No. Matt. A man called Matt.'

'Oh! Erm, no, I don't think so. Why?'

'She left him the shop downstairs.'

'Oh! Mr Conrad. Yes. She mentioned him once or twice, mostly I saw his name in the paperwork. Why? Have you met him? What's he like?'

'Matt Conrad,' Lilah murmured to herself. 'She didn't call him Matt?'

'She might have done, I don't really remember.'

'But she didn't mention him much?'

'No. Why? She told me she was splitting the flat and the shop, that you would get the flat, and the shop would go to the man currently renting it.'

'No reason. I just wondered. You know, because I met him.'

'What's he like? Is he nice?'

'Very,' Lilah said automatically. 'I can see why Lillian left him the shop.'

'How old is he?'

'My sort of age.'

'Oh, I assumed he'd be older.'

Lilah frowned.

'How come?'

'I don't know. I always assumed Lillian had a thing for him. Maybe he was her lover.'

An image of Matt flashed in front of Lilah's eyes

and she shook her head.

'Maybe. I don't think so, though. But maybe.' She remembered how shy he'd been, how he'd stumbled over his words. 'He was at her funeral.'

'He was?'

'He's Gorgeous Funeral Man.'

Lilah's mother gasped and then burst out laughing.

'All right. Not Lillian's lover, then. I hope.'

'Why you hope?'

'Because she would have told me if she'd managed to convince a much younger man into bed with her. I hope she would have told me. Why wouldn't she have told me?'

Lilah smiled.

'No, you're right. She would have told you. The way Bea tells it, Lillian was a real flirt in the local art community, so I imagine if she had a lover, he would be another artist.'

'Good word, lover.'

Lilah agreed, still thinking about Matt.

'Well, if you think this Matt is gorgeous, maybe Lillian meant him for you.'

'Mum, I don't think that's how life works. Lillian was just doing a good thing for Matt by leaving him the shop, just like she did a good thing for me, leaving me the flat. That's all.'

'True. Well, if you meet a Guy or a Stan, or Bea mentions them, you let me know. Those were the names Lillian mentioned the most, often a little wistfully. Stan especially. But, yes, also Guy.'

'Aguy. What's an aguy?' Lilah asked, smirking.

'Not aguy, a guy called Guy.' She could hear her mother beaming down the phone.

Lilah laughed and told her mother more about the Christmas decorations going up, about gossip Bea had given her, about how the waves had looked the day before.

'I was about to go out and look at the sea,' she told her mother. 'I can send you a video?'

'Yes, please! We'll have to come visit when you get the second bedroom cleared. Or we could stay in a hotel, that way we don't have to cook.'

'I can cook for you.'

'Yes, but someone gets paid to clean up at a hotel. A much better arrangement.'

'Okay. I'll send you a video. And hey, Mum, if you do want me home earlier, you just have to say.'

'I know. Thank you. Love you.'

'Love you too.'

Lilah hung up and stared at her blank phone. She knew if she wanted to go home earlier, her parents would welcome her with open arms. There was a part of her that felt so guilty not going home, but the truth was that she didn't want to. She wanted to be there for her mother in her grief, but she was already home. This was home now. And she wanted to make it more of a home.

Lilah went back to her coat, and as she slid one arm inside, her bladder pointed out to her that it was rather full and there had better be a toilet wherever she was going. Sighing, pulling her coat off, cursing the cup of coffee, she rushed to the bathroom. As she was washing her hands, she checked her reflection in the mirror over the sink out of habit and saw a figure standing behind her, next to the bath.

Heart in her throat, Lilah squealed and span round. It all happened in seconds. There wasn't enough time to work out if it was an intruder or a friendly face. How could it be a friendly face?

There was no one there.

Slowly, Lilah checked the room, which didn't take long as it was so small and there was just the toilet, sink and the bath with a shower over it. She slowly turned back to look at her reflection. Maybe the shower curtain looked like someone standing behind her.

It didn't.

There was no one in the reflection other than herself.

Heart still pounding, Lilah stepped out of the bathroom and stopped to listen.

'Hello?' she called out, her voice breaking.

No one answered.

Because no one was there.

Rushing to the front door, Lilah grabbed her phone, keys, coat and boots. She waited until the front door was closed behind her before she pulled on the boots and coat, locked the door and checked the shop window.

The light was on, but she couldn't see Matt. Maybe it had been him. Maybe he'd made his way inside somehow. No, no, there he was, walking out from the back with a customer to the counter, holding some books, chatting, laughing, to the counter. He didn't glance up, so she checked her front door was locked and took a deep breath to steady herself, before heading out to the road and down to the sea.

The lights weren't turned on yet and the town was slipping into the dark grey of a dull December afternoon. The wind, on the other hand, was sharp and laced with ice. It blasted across her face, twisting in her hair until she found a woolly hat in her pocket and pulled it down over her ears. Beneath the hat, further down in the pocket, were gloves which she gratefully yanked over her cold fingers. Then she shoved her gloved hands into her pockets and blew back at the wind.

The ocean was angry this afternoon. The waves large, rolling forward and crashing against the sand. A couple of dog walkers were braving its wrath, the dogs running joyously after thrown balls, sniffing among the seaweed and shells.

Lilah stayed on the esplanade, buffeted by the wind, facing out to sea but with concrete under her boots instead of sand.

After a moment, she took out her phone and filmed the waves, before sending the video to her mother with a kiss. Then she found a bench and sat to continue watching the ocean. Each roll of the waves seemed to reverberate through her, washing up the anger and fear and sadness that were mixed inside her and throwing it up against the walls of her stomach and chest. It mixed and broiled until it was up in her throat. Until the hot tears started to come. They had to be hot, because every other part of her was so cold.

She cried silently at the angry waves, until she could barely breathe. Thankfully, due to the cold wind pricking at her eyes and nose on every walk, she'd stuffed some tissues into her coat pocket the previous day. Lilah blew her nose and dabbed her eyes and wondered how red and puffy she looked. She wondered if she cared.

This was the time to go home, but she found her legs unwilling to move. She didn't want to go home.

She had imagined the figure in the bathroom, she was sure of it. But what if she was wrong? Her gut was telling her it had been real. If it was real, where had the person gone? Swallowing hard on her dry throat, Lilah considered her options. Then, her legs agreeing, she stood and made her way to the local coffee shop.

11

The shop was empty but Matt couldn't close up yet. The local schools would be letting out soon, which meant some of the students would pop in for their latest comics and graphic novels, or a browse, or to meet up with friends. At that moment, though, the shop was silent. He considered, not for the first time, whether he should set up a sound system to have background music playing.

He was looking up at the walls, trying to work out how to install such a thing, when the bell above the door rang. Lilah bustled in with two takeaway coffee cups and a thin smile.

'Hi.' She stopped in front of the counter. 'What coffee do you like?'

'Latte?' he ventured, looking her up and down.

She was bundled up against the cold, her hair poking out wildly from beneath her hat, her eyes wide and wilder. She handed him one of the coffee cups and he took it tentatively. 'Thank you?'

'I'm sorry about yesterday,' she said matter-of-factly. 'I was perhaps a little harsh.'

'Oh, no, I was going to knock on your door later. I wanted to apologise. I was way out of line. I'm so sorry. Can we please forget I said all that?'

The corner of Lilah's mouth twitched and she nodded, finally smiling properly.

'Okay, yes. Good. Yes. Let's start again. Hi, I'm Lilah.' She held out her free hand.

Something inside Matt twisted pleasurably.

'Hi. Matt.'

They shook hands, his warm, hers a freezing woollen glove she'd forgotten to take off.

'So, you've moved into the flat upstairs, huh?' he continued.

'Yeah. And you own the shop downstairs.'

'Sounds like we need our own sitcom.'

Lilah laughed and there was that pleasurable twist inside Matt again. He ignored it as best he could.

There was a pause as they smiled at one another, and then Lilah cleared her throat.

'I don't suppose I can ask you a favour?'

Matt's smile dropped, but only for a moment and then he plastered it back in place.

'What kind of favour?' he asked, studying his coffee. He'd thought it a peace offering, but maybe it was more of a bribe.

'I saw something strange in the flat earlier and I'm... Well, I'm scared to go back in.'

Matt looked up at her, still frowning but now for

a different reason.

'What was it?'

'I don't know. But I swear I saw someone behind me when I looked in the mirror. When I turned around there was no one there. And it was in the bathroom, which is tiny. There's nowhere to hide and I was next to the door.'

Matt glanced sideways to the back of his shop, where the crashing noises kept coming from. Where he'd seen the outline of a woman.

'Hmm.'

'I think I just need a friendly human to come check it out with me,' Lilah continued, oblivious to his suspicions.

'Yeah. Of course. Lead the way.' Matt gestured for her to go to the flat's front door. He followed her out of the shop, locked up behind him and, coffee in hand, led Lilah through the front door and up the stairs.

The flat still smelled of Lillian, although it was mingling with what was probably Lilah. Everything else was pretty much the same, though. The same furniture, the same colour on the walls, the same pictures and artwork. The scuff where he'd helped Lillian drag a dresser upstairs, had fallen and been pinned against the wall by the hefty thing.

Matt hesitated at the top of the stairs, taking it all in, and he pushed down the yawning hole of grief that had opened up in his gut. He looked again, this time for shadows that shouldn't be there.

Hiding behind him, Lilah gripped her coffee, moving to stand just a little too close. Enough that it became hard to concentrate. Which was ridiculous, as if he hadn't stood close to a woman before. As if women in the checkout queues at the supermarket had any idea of personal space. They didn't make it difficult to concentrate. Actually, if Matt was being honest, they did a little, but only because there was never any reason for people to stand so close together. It was tricky remembering how tills worked when someone was breathing down your neck.

This wasn't like that. Instead of annoyance, the closeness of Lilah was distracting in other ways. Ways that Matt didn't wish to dwell on, because it would only add yet another layer of complexity to this whole thing.

He made his way to the bathroom first, poking his head around the door. It was empty and there was nowhere to hide, although he checked behind the shower curtain and resisted the urge to check inside the toilet.

'What did they look like?' he whispered, just in case.

Lilah gave this some thought as Matt backed out of the bathroom and considered where to go next. She helped him decide by leading him to the second bedroom. Lillian had always kept it clear, in case of guests. Now it was full of boxes with unfamiliar handwriting scrawled over them. They were Lilah's possessions, he guessed.

'A dark shadow,' she murmured. 'A woman,' she said after another moment of thought.

'Hmm.'

'You think I'm making it up?'

'No, I'm wondering if it's the same woman I saw in my shop.' Matt glanced back to her and then dropped to the floor, checking under the bed. When he re-emerged, Lilah was staring at him.

'What do you mean?'

'There was a woman in my shop. But I didn't see her come in, the bell didn't ring, and it wasn't exactly busy. The shop was empty, but I didn't notice her. She was standing at the back and I looked away for a second, trying to work out how she got in. Then when I looked again, she was gone. But no one passed me, the bell didn't ring, nothing.' Matt brushed down his jeans. The room was empty. 'Have you had anything fall over? Any weird noises?' For a moment there, it sounded like he knew what he was talking about.

'No. None. Except the box of Lillian's art supplies fell on me. But I was moving things around so that was probably my own fault. Despite not moving anything near it,' said Lilah, drifting off and meeting Matt's gaze. 'You don't think it's...'

Matt mentally shook himself.

'No. Nah. No, can't be. Right? I'm sure it's nothing.'

'Probably the grief,' Lilah murmured.

'Yeah. Probably.'

'For both of us.'

'Yup.'

'In Lillian's home and the shop she loved so much.'

Matt glanced at Lilah out of the corner of his eye.

'I'll check the rest of the flat, though. Just in case. And if it helps,' he added, 'I'm just downstairs if you need me.'

'Yeah, until you shut up shop and go home.'

Matt blew out his cheeks.

'Right. Well, there's a DnD game tomorrow night, so there'll be a few of us around late then.'

Lilah's eyes lit up.

'I've never played DnD. I've always wanted to give it a try.'

'Really? Well, great. I have a new campaign starting in January, if you're interested.'

'Yeah, I'd like that. Put me down.' Lilah grinned at him. It took Matt a moment to remember why he was there, pull himself out of getting lost in Lilah's eyes and smile back.

Muttering to himself, he checked the rest of the flat: kitchen, living room, Lilah's bedroom that still felt a lot like Lillian's. He averted his gaze when he spotted clothes on the bed, just in case he saw something she didn't want him to.

Then he returned to the living room, hands on his hips.

'Seems clear.'

Lilah sighed.

'Thankfully. Thank you so much for checking for me, and for taking me seriously.'

'Of course. Everyone should feel safe in their home.' Matt rubbed the back of his neck, thinking of his sleeping bag downstairs.

He started to move, heading back to the stairs that led down to the front door, when Lilah stopped him.

'I thought about what you said. About Lillian promising you the flat.'

'Oh, I—'

'I felt bad about it, and wanted to check, so I went through all of my paperwork.'

'So did I, and—'

'And then I emailed Lillian's solicitor.'

Matt stopped and waited to see if Lilah would continue. She paused, long enough for him to sigh and step closer to her.

'Thank you,' he started. 'That's... It's very kind of you, but I sort of did the same and I found... Well, I found a letter from Lillian.'

'Oh?' Lilah stepped closer.

'Yeah, I don't know why I didn't see it before. It must have been hidden among other stuff, or something. I don't know. But it explains everything. She apologises for going back on her promise, which I'm sort of glad about. Was beginning to think I'd gone mad, misremembering and being an arse about it.'

Lilah smiled.

'I was going to mention it, but then the coffee and the...' Matt waved his arms, gesturing at the flat as a whole.

'The Thing That Shall Not Be Named?' Lilah offered.

'Pretty sure she likes to be called Lillian.'

They stared at one another, Lilah's eyes widening slightly as they smiled, both trying not to laugh.

'Do you think...' Lilah closed the gap between her and Matt, and Matt did his best to breathe like a normal person. 'Do you think it is her?'

'I hope so,' he whispered back. 'Wouldn't like to think what else it is.'

Lilah's smile faltered and for a moment they stayed there, a little too close, searching one another's eyes, Matt glancing down to her lips for the briefest of moments. Then he ripped his gaze away, stepped back and made for the stairs.

'I'd best go.'

'Oh.'

'Oh?' Matt hesitated, looking back to her, wondering what he might have missed.

'Is the shop open late tonight?'

'No,' he replied, having considered his options.

'I wondered if you're busy?'

Matt almost laughed but swallowed it instead.

'Doing what?' he croaked.

Lilah shrugged.

'This is your hometown. You have a life here. I don't know. I'd really like to see the Christmas lights, all lit up, and it's been too windy and rainy until tonight.'

Matt glanced to the window at the dull December light.

'Okay.'

A little too quickly, Lilah asked, 'Do you fancy getting a coffee and going to see them with me?' She pressed her lips together to keep any more words in.

Matt went to say yes, but then stopped. She seemed so nervous; was she asking him out? He hesitated a little too long, his mouth opening and closing.

'It's okay if you're busy. I just thought it might be good to get to know each other, seeing as how I'll be living on top of you – I mean, upstairs.' Lilah looked down at the floor and Matt smiled before quickly wiping it away.

'Yeah. Sounds good.' He put his hands in his pockets, then realised how stupid that must look and took them out. 'I shut the shop at five, I'll knock on your door then?'

That was what he used to say to Lillian, whenever she needed help with something. *I'll knock on your door*. Matt swallowed hard on the lump rising in his throat and pushed the sadness back down.

'Great. I'll, erm, try not to think about what else

might be in this flat until then,' said Lilah, glancing around the room.

'See you then. Bye, Lillian!' Matt called, and Lilah shot him a look.

He left laughing to himself, trotting down the stairs, opening the front door to find a group of teenagers in uniform outside his shop. He greeted them, let them in, and as he walked through his own front door, whispered, 'Hi, Lillian.'

12

The flat was eerily quiet with Matt gone. Lilah could hardly bare it. She stood still for a moment, her mind blank with panic, and then she shook it away. The flat was empty other than her, and Matt was only downstairs. Everything was fine. She pulled out her phone and found a Christmas playlist that looked good, then she took the phone and music, playing loud, into the second bedroom. Somewhere in there she'd seen a box marked 'XMAS DECS'.

She found it again easily, hidden in the corner of the wardrobe, covered by Lillian's old winter coats. Carrying it into the living room, she sat on the floor and opened it. A waft of Christmas along with a wisp of Lillian's scent drifted out of it and Lilah breathed it in. Then she slowly pulled out the decorations. Two boxes of fairy lights, some colourful baubles, a little pile of old tinsel, and a small plastic wreath presumably for the front door. At the bottom was a wooden box, inside of which was a load of tissue paper. Lilah went through it carefully and found a glass angel, a glittery star and another bauble. She held the bauble up to the dwindling afternoon light and smiled, her chest tightening. Swallowing on a painful lump in her throat, Lilah let the glass bauble holding the photograph of Lillian holding a baby Lilah, toddler Emily by her side, slowly turn before she cupped it and held it close to her chest.

'I didn't know you had this,' she whispered to the room. When she looked back up, her eyes glistened with unspent tears. 'I really hope it is you that's here and not something else.' She gave a soft laugh at herself and rubbed her eyes. 'Guess I need to buy a Christmas tree before I put these up. Matt will know where from, right? Right. And now I've smudged my makeup.'

Lilah sighed and placed the bauble carefully back into its tissue paper and box. Before doing anything else, she attempted to string one box of fairy lights around the living room window that looked out onto the road, using the clips she'd found in the box and a bit of tape, just to be certain. It involved standing on the arm of the sofa and reaching too far one way, then finding a chair to stand on for the other side, almost slipping in her socks. Whether they'd still be up when she came home that evening was debateable, but for now, Lilah had pretty twinkling fairy lights around her window.

It was a start.

There was just enough time to smarten herself up. Despite Matt having already seen her that day, she jumped in the hot shower and washed her hair, blow-drying it as quickly as she could. She redid her makeup, waving away any intention her body had of more tears.

'Not yet. Later,' she told it sternly.

Then she found her boots and coat, made sure she had some money on her, and waited for Matt to knock on her door. She was scrolling on her phone when the knock finally came. Glad of the interruption, Lilah jumped up and blinked a few times to reacquaint herself with the real world. Then she jogged down the stairs, grabbed her boots and coat, and opened the door.

The wind blew Matt inside.

'Oh no, has the weather turned?' Lilah cried.

The door closed behind Matt and he breathed in the stillness.

'Just a bit windy. That's more living by the coast than anything.' He shrugged it away. 'Ready?' His eyes grazed over her and Lilah did her best to ignore it while feeling every second of it, her body tingling, although that was probably the effects of the hot shower wearing off.

'Ready! And a bit hungry. How about you?'

'We can go to the coffee shop first?'

Lilah agreed and found her keys. When she straightened, Matt was smirking at her.

'Seen any more of Lillian?'

Lilah shook her head.

'No, thankfully. Well, no, not thankfully. I just…
I don't like being crept up on!' she called up the
stairs to the empty flat. 'Do you really think it's
her?' she added in a whisper to Matt, pulling on a
blue woolly hat and finding her matching gloves.

He watched her, smiling a smile that danced in
his brown eyes.

'Why not?'

'I don't know. Do you believe in all that?'

Matt shrugged.

'I don't not believe in it.'

Lilah repeated this to herself as they left the flat
and she locked the front door behind her.

'Me too. I think.'

Matt shoved his hands into his coat pockets and
gestured with his head up the road.

'I know a nice coffee shop this way, unless you
had somewhere in mind?'

'Is it near the beach?'

'No. It's near an art centre.'

'Oh! I've been meaning to go there.'

They walked side by side, falling into easy step
with one another, up the road and to the left, away
from the beach. The conversation came easy, even
when they had to go single file along the narrowing
pavement.

'How was your afternoon?'

'Usual,' said Matt. 'My regulars came in after
school.'

'Are they kids?'

'Those ones are. But generally the regulars are all ages.'

'I noticed! Those men in suits—'

'They work in an office across town.'

'—and that older man.'

'Stanley. He knew Lillian, by the way. He's an interesting guy.' Matt gave Lilah a sideways look

'Were they friends?' Lilah asked slowly, trying to think why the name 'Stanley' gave her pause.

Matt laughed.

'Oh.' Lilah blinked hurriedly. 'Were they more than friends? You know, Lillian never talked about relationships. I often wondered if she was a lesbian. I got a little excited when I met her painting friend, Bea, but it turns out they were just friends.'

'Sorry, as far as I'm aware, Lillian was into men.'

'Into this Stanley?' she gasped. 'Stan? She mentioned a Stan to my mum.'

'I couldn't possibly say.' Matt grinned, leading her down a side road, away from the traffic. Either side of them were medieval buildings rendered pink on the left and white on the right, and ahead was the timber and stone structure of an old mill. Lilah paused to take it in.

'Wow.'

Above the front door to the mill were the words 'Arts Centre', and at the windows were paintings and sculptures. Off to the left was a boutique shop and an obvious artist workshop, and to the right was a café with tables outside and a canopy set up to protect them from the rain. The canopy was decorated with tasteful lights and between each building were criss-crossing lightbulbs on a string, swinging in the wind. Each building had its own Christmas tree, one lit up with green lights, one with blue and one with warm white. Between the shop and the mill was a small path, leading into what looked like trees and a growing darkness.

'Where's the water?' Lilah asked. If there was a mill, there had to be water.

Matt pointed to the side where a low concrete wall was attached to the nearest medieval building.

'It goes under the road we just came from and then through there.' He pointed to the darkening path beyond the mill to the trees. 'The mill wheel is on the other side. Drink?'

'Absolutely,' Lilah breathed, stepping away to look over the concrete wall to the dark, rushing water below. It was heading out to the ocean and a couple of pigeons sitting on a ledge looked up at her quizzically.

'Hi,' she told them, before ducking back and catching up to Matt.

He held the door open for her and she was immediately hit by the warmth of the café, the scent of coffee and cinnamon filling the room. Lilah pulled off her woolly hat and gloves, and unzipped her coat, suddenly far too warm.

'What would you like?' Matt asked, walking up to

the counter and display of cakes and pastries kept behind glass.

There were the remains of two large cakes, a pile of mince pies, a few remaining muffins and two croissants. Lilah stared at each of them in turn.

'The mince pies are fresh,' said the woman behind the counter, grinning at Matt.

'Great, I'll have a mince pie and a regular latte, please. Lilah?'

'Oh, erm...'

'You can have the cake if you want,' he urged, his eyes sparkling, although that could have been the reflection of the fairy lights festooned around the counter.

'Yeah?'

'Yeah, we're not in a hurry. Are we?'

'No. Nope. Okay.' Lilah turned to the woman behind the counter. 'Can I have a slice of the chocolate cake, please? And a cappuccino. Thanks.'

The woman brought it all up on the till and both Matt and Lilah reached for the cards on their phones. They stopped when they both went to pay.

'This is on me,' said Matt. 'Because of earlier. An apology cake.'

'What? No! I wouldn't have ordered the cake if I knew you were paying.'

'Why not?'

'It's too expensive.'

Matt laughed.

'It's not expensive.'

'No, but you know what I mean. It's more than a mince pie.'

'It's fine. I wanted you to get the cake. I saw you eyeing it up.'

'But—'

'Please, this is on me.'

'But I'm apologising too.'

Matt shrugged and went to pay, holding out his arm to block Lilah in case she tried anything. She relented.

'Fine, and thank you, but I'm getting it next time.' She grinned at the look Matt gave her, and her insides warmed at the raised eyebrow the woman behind the till gave him.

Matt suggested a table by the window. They huddled around the table for two, Lilah staring out into the darkness, the Christmas lights dotted like stars in the clear night sky.

'This is so beautiful. I had no idea this was here. I mean, I knew it existed somewhere. I didn't realise it was so close.'

'Hmm. Lillian had some art up in the gallery, last I heard.'

Lilah snapped round to look at him with wide eyes.

'What? She never told us that.'

'I feel like there's a lot she didn't tell you?'

Something inside Lilah deflated and she sat back.

'I guess.' She looked out the window again, only

to be brought back to the world by the woman bringing over their coffees, cake and mince pie. They thanked her and the woman left them, grinning to herself. 'Do you know her?' Lilah whispered, picking up her fork and sliding it into the cake. The ease with which it went in made her stomach growl.

'Yeah. That's Rachel. We went to school together.'

'Oh. Did you and her...?'

'No, no. We never talked at school. But she runs this place with her sister-in-law, so we got talking one day, as business owners, you know? And she kept inviting me to the Chambers of Commerce meetings. So now we're sort of business friends.'

'That's nice.'

'Not really. The Chambers of Commerce meetings start at half seven in the morning and they're so mind-numbingly boring I actually fell asleep at the last one I went to. Haven't been back since.'

Lilah laughed and wrapped her defrosting fingers around the cappuccino mug.

'Noted. Don't go to those meetings.'

'They did a nice full English breakfast, though.'

'Oh, really?'

Matt grinned and took a big bite from his mince pie. Lilah sampled her cake, moaned accidentally and then shoved a forkful of it into her mouth.

'Good cake?' Matt grinned.

Lilah nodded.

'Thank you. I definitely owe you.'

Matt waved her away.

'I'm just glad we're on good terms now. No hard feelings or anything.'

'No. I get it. I'm sorry Lillian didn't tell you, or that you didn't find the letter before, I guess. She should have told you in person.'

'Maybe she was too ill then,' Matt offered.

'I do wonder why she didn't really mention you, towards the end, I mean. When she was living with us.'

'Did she mention me at all?'

Lilah shrugged.

'She just told my mum about the man who rented the shop from her and how nice he was. Is.'

Matt sat up a little straighter.

'That's nice. Wonder why she didn't say more.'

'No idea. She didn't talk much towards the end. Maybe it was that.'

'But you didn't know about me before? Weren't you close with her before? Close enough for her to leave you her flat.'

Lilah played with her cake, gently stabbing her fork into it and cutting it into bitesize pieces.

'We hadn't spoken for a while. Years. I used to visit all the time, especially as a teenager. Then I had a rocky twenties. Went travelling, went out with awful men, lost a couple of jobs, changed career path. By my late twenties, I was more settled and I visited some more. And then I got a new job and I... stopped.' She frowned. 'It wasn't intentional. Everything just got so busy.'

'I'm sure she understood,' Matt murmured.

'Yeah. I hope so. By the time she'd come to live with us, I'd lost it all. The job, that is. The career. I was back home living with my parents, and then with Lillian, but she was so sick. We caught up at the beginning, before she went really downhill. I guess that's why she left me the flat without telling me. Maybe she'd been meaning to tell me, and tell you about the flat, but her voice went before she could. And then her energy. That letter might have been written between that, maybe just after her voice started to go. It would have hurt her to call you, hurt her throat, I mean, so she wrote the letter and then didn't have the energy. That makes sense.'

Matt only nodded.

'Guess it doesn't matter now,' he said when Lilah didn't say more. 'Best just to get on with it.'

'Yeah.' Lilah's mind was filled with those last days of Lillian's life. Slowly, she brought herself back to the café and shoved one of the pieces of cake she'd cut into her mouth, sipping her coffee. 'When does the gallery open?' she asked after swallowing.

'Oh, most days. I'm sure it'll be back open tomorrow morning.'

'I'll have to go look to see if anything Lillian did is still there.'

'Good idea.'

Matt's voice had gone soft, quiet, distant. Lilah

watched him, a small panic rising inside. Had she said something wrong? She cleared her throat.

'Whereabouts do you live? Is it nearby? Walkable to the shop?'

Matt blinked and then nodded.

'Yeah, it's walkable.'

Lilah waited, but he didn't give any more information.

'Okay. Do you live with someone?'

'Like who?'

'I don't know. A girlfriend, boyfriend, wife, husband, housemate?'

Matt smiled.

'None of the above. No. It's just me.'

'That's quite a feat in this town, isn't it?'

A cloud passed over Matt's features.

'Yeah. So, are we going to go look at Christmas lights? There's a little trail from here to the high street and down to the front.'

Lilah scooped up the last of her cake, studying him, trying to work out which question or statement had gone too far.

'Sure.'

They left the café behind, Matt holding the door open for Lilah again, and wandered back to the road, Matt pointing out certain lights as they went. It wasn't just the lights hanging over the road, between the buildings, each shop also had a lit-up display or its own special Christmas tree.

'I need to get a tree,' Lilah murmured, admiring

one small potted tree decorated florescent blue. 'Where do you buy your Christmas trees around here?'

'The supermarket?' Matt offered.

'Oh.'

Matt smiled at her, leading her to the next window display.

'There's a place by the town football club, all the proceeds go to the team Danny coaches. Danny's my mate – we went to school together. He'll kill me if he finds out I told you to go to a supermarket.'

Lilah nodded, smiling.

'That secret will die with me.'

Matt gave her a strange look and then burst out laughing. For a moment, he held out his hand and she almost instinctively took it. Then he seemed to remember himself and pulled away. She followed him onwards, smiling to herself.

The trail wasn't as long as she thought. They ended up back at the flat and shop within an hour. Lilah invited Matt up but he declined, said he had some work to do, and vanished into the shop, the door closing as Lilah suggested he come up afterwards. A little deflated, Lilah let herself into the flat and went about her evening, alone. She went to bed late, knowing she'd regret it, and closed her eyes thinking about how the next day she'd go buy a tree and support the local football team.

Sleep came quickly and she dreamt she was sitting in the living room when a woman walked in, smiling down at her. She didn't look sick anymore, and she was younger, a paintbrush in one hand which she offered to Lilah. Lilah took it tentatively, and Lillian said, 'Hello, Lilah, I'm sorry I scared you.'

13

'It's okay,' Matt told Lillian.

They were sitting in his shop, her on the armchair Stanley usually claimed, him on the stool behind the counter. He'd offered her a drink and she'd reminded him that she was dead. Surely, he'd suggested, even ghosts could drink in a dream. Lillian had been intrigued, so Matt had tried dreaming up a coffee and Lillian had attempted to sip it. It needed more milk.

'It's not okay. It's not okay at all. I left specific instructions with my solicitor to give you that letter and he ignored me.'

'Or it just got lost. Anyway, it's fine.'

'It's not fine. You and Lilah argued about it!'

'But it's fine now. Anyway, who cares if I argue with Lilah?'

'I do.'

Matt stared at Lillian. She was younger and there was more colour in her cheeks than she'd had when they'd last seen each other. As the disease had progressed, Lillian had become withdrawn, disappearing into her flat for days, only answering messages and not calls. Then she'd left, with only a quick goodbye.

'Why didn't you tell me you weren't coming back?' Matt asked quietly, unable to look at her.

'Oh. My dear boy.' Lillian moved from the chair to the counter, reaching out to brush surprisingly warm fingers across his cheek. 'I had such plans for you. But sometimes Death comes when you're not ready, when you still have so much to do. I still had so much to do. I was angry and resentful, and I didn't want you to see me like that. I didn't know that it would be the...' Lillian took a deep breath and smiled at Matt, her eyes watery. 'I didn't want to accept it would be the last.'

He reached out and squeezed her hand. 'You gave me so much when you didn't have to.'

Lillian grinned.

'I saw in you what I always wanted someone to see in me.'

'Oh yeah? What was that?' Matt smiled back.

'Potential.' Lillian looked around the shop. 'You have no idea how capable you are.'

'Ha!'

'I mean it, Matthew,' said Lillian, her tone suddenly sharp and serious. 'You need to embrace who you are, what you want, and think big.'

Matt kept smiling, although his mind was spinning.

'And how do I do that?'

Lillian opened her mouth to respond and then stopped, smiled and gave Matt a wink.

'You'll figure it out,' she whispered.

A loud beeping broke through and Matt opened his eyes, groaning, groping around for his phone to smack his alarm off. He stared blearily up at the ceiling of the shop's back room and gave a deep sigh.

By half nine, Matt was dressed, teeth cleaned, one coffee down, still wondering if he could ask Lilah for use of her shower, and eyeball deep in some admin on a spreadsheet. Sitting on the stool at his shop's counter, he stared at his laptop screen, trying to figure out what formula he needed for the job at hand.

'Must be an app for this,' he muttered, as Excel threw him an error message.

The bell above his door rang and he glanced up, then did a double take as Lilah walked in holding two cups from her kitchen. She offered one to Matt.

'Sorry, it's not a latte. Just normal coffee.'

'Good morning to you too.' Matt took the coffee with a smile. 'Thanks.'

'No problem. And good morning.' Lilah sipped her own coffee as she looked around the empty shop. 'Do you ever get customers in the morning?'

'It's Saturday.'

'In December. In a tourist town.'

Matt joined her in looking around the silent shop. He really needed to get that sound system installed, but that meant buying one first.

'I was going to buy a Christmas tree. I wondered if you cared to join me? Maybe you could get one for the shop? Every other shop has decorations up, but you don't.'

'It's barely December.'

Lilah stared at him.

'December is a week old and Christmas is in two weeks.'

Matt frowned and rubbed the back of his neck.

'That can't be right,' he mumbled, his gaze trailing back to the spreadsheet.

'Come on. Come with me. Your shop needs some Christmas, which means you need a tree.'

With a triumphant closing of his laptop, after saving the spreadsheet, Matt agreed and went to grab his coat.

'What about the coffee?' Lilah asked hesitantly.

Matt took a gulp of it and then cried out, waving at his stuck-out tongue.

'Hot!'

'Well, yeah,' Lilah laughed.

'Maybe by the time we get back, it'll be cool enough to drink,' said Matt, putting the coffee on the counter and dangling his keys from his finger. 'Let's go buy a tree before I change my mind. Before the lunchtime rush.'

Lilah took another look around the empty shop.

'Uh huh. Yup. Lunchtime rush.' She took another gulp of her coffee and placed the cup next to Matt's before following him out.

The town's football pitch was on the edge of town, flanked by allotments and with a view of the sea if you stood in the right place and on tiptoes. The Christmas trees, however, was not where the view was. They were in the car park, close to the road, and there were already a few families there choosing their trees.

'Matt! You didn't say you were coming.' Danny rushed over when he spotted Matt and Lilah walking into the car park. 'You okay?'

'Of course. What, you've never seen me buying a Christmas tree?' Matt said, distracted by the excited children helping their parents choose trees.

Danny rolled his eyes and then let his gaze land on Lilah.

'Hello, woman I've never met that Matt has brought here. Or did you just happen to come in at the same time and I've made things awkward?'

Lilah grinned and held out a hand.

'I'm Lilah. I live in the flat upstairs from Matt's shop.'

Danny's smile was frozen but his eyes widened slightly, moving to glance sideways at Matt.

'How nice to meet you,' he said, shooting Matt

another subtle look, as if he'd missed the first.

'Lilah, this is Danny. We went to school together. We played DnD all throughout our teens and always said we'd open a shop together one day, then he bailed, got a proper job, became a teacher and got married.'

'I don't remember ever saying I'd open the shop with you. I wanted to be a professional footballer. And look at me now!' Danny opened his arms wide to encompass the football club. 'Selling Christmas trees from a car park to help fund the youth team's Christmas party.'

'I thought it was fundraising for a new stand?'

'No, that's the raffle and quiz next week.'

'Huh.' Matt gazed around the Christmas trees. Surely they'd make more money from the trees than a quiz and raffle, but he didn't say anything, having no idea how much Christmas trees cost wholesale.

'It's nice to meet you, Danny,' said Lilah.

The two shook hands and smiled at one another for slightly longer than Matt liked. There was something going on between them, some unspoken words, and Matt was certain they were about him.

'So, who's looking for a tree?' Danny asked.

'Both of us,' said Lilah. 'I want a sort of medium-sized one, although it has just occurred to me I need to get it upstairs. And I guess you'll want a small one?' she asked Matt.

He shrugged.

'A little one for me, yeah. And I'll help you get yours up the stairs.'

'We both will, depending on how big the tree is, and I know just which ones to show you,' said Danny, gesturing for them to follow.

'Mates rates, though, right, Dan?'

Danny laughed over his shoulder.

'Don't let him make you buy the biggest one,' Matt whispered to Lilah. She grinned, watching Danny's back.

'I'll do my best, but you might need to save me.'

Matt laughed despite himself and then, when faced with the tallest of the trees, said, 'Nope! That won't even fit in the flat.'

'Well, I don't know how high your ceilings are,' Danny protested.

'Just a normal size tree,' Matt proclaimed, crossing his arms.

'Fine. Fine. Those there are smaller and a tad cheaper. If you don't care about the kids.'

'Don't you dare,' said Matt, holding up a finger and pointing it at his friend. 'No guilt tripping. Supermarkets don't guilt trip.'

Danny and Matt stared at one another and then burst out laughing.

'Every year,' Matt muttered, leading Lilah over to the smaller trees.

She went, watching Matt with a look of fascination that he quite liked although he wouldn't dare admit it. Lilah pulled up a tree and asked Matt to hold it so she could get a proper look.

'Hmm, no, the bottom's too bushy. How about this one? No, it's a bit uneven here. Ooh, how about this one?'

They were on their fourth tree when Matt finally found his voice and the words.

'I dreamt about Lillian last night.'

Lilah stopped and looked at him.

'Really? Me too.' She stepped closer, running a pine branch through her fingers. 'What happened in your dream?'

'She apologised that I found the letter so late.'

Lilah smiled.

'She apologised to me, too. For scaring me in the bathroom mirror.' She met Matt's eyes just as his stomach dropped. 'You think they're real? The dreams?' she whispered.

Matt shook his head, but said, 'Maybe. What do you think?'

'It felt realer than any dream I've ever had.'

Slowly, Matt met her gaze.

'Mine too.'

'How we doing over here?'

Both Matt and Lilah jumped as Danny reappeared, this time wearing thick gloves. 'Chosen a tree?'

'Uh, yeah. This one's good,' said Lilah, pointing to the tree Matt was holding. 'Just need one for Matt now.'

'Great! Let me take that, I'll put it through the

netting machine. That's my favourite bit. The little trees are over there, in pots.' Danny gestured with his head as he took the tree from Matt. 'Be careful, Lilah. Every year, Matt convinced Lillian to plant his Christmas tree in her garden. Surprised she didn't open her own farm.'

'That's not true. She only took them when I threatened to chuck them out.'

'Which is every year.'

'Yeah...'

Mind spinning, Matt followed Lilah over to the small potted trees, looking at them but not seeing them.

'Should we be worried?' he murmured.

'No. It's all for a good cause, isn't it.'

Matt blinked and then focused on Lilah.

'Not the trees,' he said. 'Lillian. Us both dreaming about her. Seeing her. Should we be worried?'

'About what?'

'That the building is haunted.'

'By Lillian. She was the nicest person in the world,' said Lilah. 'And my aunt. And she left you the shop. I don't think she's going to cause problems.'

'But what if she's stuck? Shouldn't she be, I don't know, resting in peace?'

Lilah froze, halfway down to run her fingers over a small tree. Straightening, she glanced at Matt.

'I hadn't thought of that.'

He grimaced.

'Sorry.'

'Maybe... Maybe she had unfinished business?' Lilah offered, her voice low as a family with small children appeared beside them. She pulled the tree's pot closer, looking at it from all angles. 'Isn't that why ghosts stay around?'

'I think that's just in the Casper movie.'

Lilah grinned and Matt's insides shifted pleasurably at the sight of her trying not to laugh. He'd done that. He kept doing that, and each time he made her smile, it sent a warm wave of pleasure through him. That couldn't be good. He pushed the thought away.

'Well, this one's nice,' said Lilah, bringing Matt back to the present situation.

He gave the tree a quick look, said, 'Yup,' and picked the tree up, almost instantly regretting it. 'Where's Danny?' he asked in a strained voice.

'This way.' Lilah touched his arm, and it took everything Matt had to not drop the tree. 'Are you okay?'

'Hmm.'

Lilah quickly guided Matt through the trees to Danny who was having far too much fun shoving people's freshly bought trees through the netting machine.

'I'm so tempted to put myself through it,' he told them as Matt tried to slowly lower the pot to the ground without dropping it. 'Fancy going through?'

Matt realised Danny was talking to him and gave the machine a suspicious look.

'No?'

'Thought you'd say that.'

'I know. I'm just no fun.'

Danny barked a laugh and gave them Lilah's netted tree, writing down the costs of both hers and Matt's potted tree in a notepad he got from another of the football coaches working there.

'How're you getting them home?' he asked as Lilah paid before Matt could attempt to argue, given that he was still out of breath from carrying the pot. He'd pay her back later.

'Oh.' Lilah glanced at Matt. 'Didn't think about that. Why did we walk here instead of drive?'

Danny looked between them and raised an eyebrow.

'Want a lift?'

Matt nodded, still breathing hard.

'And in exchange for petrol money, you'll come to the fundraising quiz. It's Christmas themed.'

Matt couldn't think of anything worse than a Christmas-themed quiz, but he was in no position to argue, and anyway, Lilah got there first again.

'Great! Thank you so much. It's not far by car.'

'Just awkward,' Matt managed, flashing Danny a grin.

14

The Christmas tree was decorated alone, in her flat, but to loud Christmas music as she talked to Lillian, so at no point did Lilah feel alone. It helped knowing that Matt was just below her, decorating his own tree.

'It would have been nice to do this together. Maybe I should have offered to help him so he would have to return the favour,' she murmured, moving a bauble and stepping back to decide if she liked the new position. All the Christmas décorations were Lillian's, so it made sense to include her.

Not that Lillian was necessarily talking back. At least, not in the conventional sense. This wasn't like the dream, where Lillian was in front of her as if still alive, talking as she had before the disease had progressed. Instead, there was a chill in the flat, and then a tingling warmth. That warmth fell over Lilah's right hand at that moment, as she reached for the bauble again. She pulled her hand back: Lillian was happy with the placement.

'Should I ask him out on a proper date?' Lilah continued, reaching for the next bauble. 'I don't even know how to do that. Do you know, the last time I asked a man out, I tripped over my words, gave up, tried to run away and then actually tripped over my own foot. And he said no. After all that.' She sighed. 'Should I just ask him out for a drink? Seems silly when we're going to have drinks at that quiz. How about here?' she asked, placing the bauble on a branch. Her hand tingled with warmth and Lilah nodded, reaching for the next one.

'Okay.' She turned to the room. 'Lillian, should I ask Matt out?'

The air didn't appear to change or move, but the song that was playing skipped, which shouldn't happen considering it was streaming on Lilah's phone. Although maybe the internet connection had blipped. 'Was that a yes? Do it again for yes,' Lilah checked.

The song skipped again.

'I was afraid of that,' Lilah murmured, sitting on the sofa and looking up at the tree. It was coming along nicely. There were only a few decorations left and then something to go on the top. It wasn't the time for sitting down, but Lilah had already sat, her stomach giddy with the idea that she was talking to the ghost of her aunt and her aunt was *responding*.

What was she supposed to do with that? Shouldn't she be scared? Or, at least, more scared than she was.

'Okay. I'll ask him out. But maybe not yet. Maybe we need to get Christmas out of the way first,' Lilah decided. 'Plus, we're neighbours. What if it all goes wrong?'

The song skipped again and Lilah stared at her phone. 'What does that mean?' she asked it in a whisper.

The music stopped and Lilah's stomach twisted in a shot of fear. Reaching out, she went to try starting it again when her phone burst to life, ringing and flashing the name of her mother.

Hand on her chest, breathing hard, Lilah answered with a quiet, 'Hello?'

'Hi! Are you all right? What's wrong? Why are you so quiet?'

'Are you all right? Is Dad all right?'

'Of course! What's going on?'

Lilah sat back and breathed deeply, waiting for the anxiety to leach away.

'Nothing's wrong. I'm fine.'

'Why were you so quiet?'

'I—' Lilah looked around the room. Could she tell her mother about Lillian? 'I was just decorating the tree and had music on loud, so you scared me. That's all.'

'Oh, how lovely. How's the tree looking?'

'Good.' Lilah grinned up at the tree.

'Is it big?'

'Yeah.'

'How did you get it home?'

'Oh, Matt's friend who sold me the tree gave us a lift back and helped me get it up the stairs. And by helped me, I mean he and Matt carried it up the stairs for me.'

'Nice to know two strong, kind men.'

'It is.'

'What's his friend like?'

'Incredibly handsome with a wife, a child and one on the way.'

'Ah.'

'Matt's handsome too,' Lilah added without thinking, and then snapped her mouth shut.

There was a pause down the phone.

'Is there something there?'

'Maybe. I don't know.'

'But you'd like there to be?'

Lilah stared at the tree, trying not to think about Matt.

'Did you just call for a chat or was there something?' she asked after a moment, snapping away from her thoughts, suddenly desperate to change the conversation.

'There was a reason.' Her mother stopped and silence filled Lilah's ear for a moment. 'What was it.'

Lilah waited. Her mother started sucking on her teeth as she thought, the sound making Lilah's eye twitch.

'Don't worry. It'll come back to you. Maybe—'

'That was it! Christmas.'

Lilah blinked.

'Yes?'

'We're coming to yours for Christmas.'

That silence returned, but this time it was on Lilah's end as she stared at the tree, seeing through it, her mouth open.

'Hello? Are you still there?'

'I'm here,' said Lilah uncertainly. 'Erm, that's... great! When are you coming? Who's coming?'

'Just me and your dad, there's only one other bedroom, after all.'

'Oh, you're staying here. With me.'

'Yes!'

'Okay.' Lilah looked over her shoulder to the door of the second bedroom. 'That room's still full of boxes.'

'But there's a bed in there, isn't there?'

'There is.'

'A double bed, right?'

'Right.'

'So, pile the boxes in a corner and we'll be fine. Don't worry.'

'Pile the... Right. Yup.'

'We'll bring some food with us. We can make Christmas dinner together in Lillian's kitchen. It'll be like she's there with us.'

Something inside Lilah collapsed and she relented, sinking into the sofa.

'That's a really nice idea, Mum. Sounds great. When are you coming?'

'We'll come up Christmas Eve Eve. Or maybe Eve Eve Eve.'

Lilah repeated that, counting on her fingers.

'Okay. No problem. Where will you park? There's only one parking space.'

'Don't you worry. We'll get twenty-four hour tickets at the public car park up the road. We don't mind.'

Lilah was about to remind her mother that she really didn't mind going home for Christmas, but stopped when she remembered that wouldn't change anything. This was Lillian's home, and Lilah knew for a fact she was here, although she wasn't about to tell her mother that in case it upset her.

'Sounds good, Mum.'

'And then maybe we can meet this Matt!'

Lilah went cold.

'Oh, erm...'

'I'm sure he'll be off celebrating Christmas with his family, though, right? His shop will be shut. Unless he gets much Christmas trade?'

'I don't know,' said Lilah weakly.

'We'll find out!' She could hear her mother beaming down the phone. 'Don't you worry about a thing, just make sure those boxes are piled up and maybe clean bedding, hmm? We'll do the rest.'

'Right. I mean, I can get food...'

'Well, yes, buy the food you want, but we can bring most of it. Don't you worry. It'll be Christmas away from home. And I'll get to see the sea! I can't wait. Maybe we'll come earlier.'

'Ha, okay.' Lilah swallowed hard on her constricting throat and then closed her eyes, trying to relax. 'Okay. Well, you let me know.'

'Yes, of course. And you're okay?'

'I'm good, Mum.'

'Good. I'll let you get back to your tree décorating.'

'Thanks.'

They said their goodbyes and Lilah hung up, lowering her phone and staring at the tree.

'Well, there you go.'

She daren't look around at the rest of the flat, filled with boxes, Lillian's things mixing with her own possessions. She'd wanted to go through everything slowly, meaningfully, but if her mother came then she'd want to do it in a hurry. Would seeing so much of Lillian's stuff still out hurt her, remind her too much of the sister she'd lost?

Lilah groaned and laid her head back on the sofa.

So much for the gentle, easy Christmas before the drive back to her parents. At least she wouldn't need to drive, and if she needed a break, she could always walk down to the sea.

Smiling, Lilah looked back to the tree and prepared to lift herself from the sofa to finish decorating.

'Your sister's coming for Christmas,' she told Lillian, pressing play on the Christmas music. 'This flat's going to get very full, very quickly.'

15

It didn't take long for Matt to decorate his little potted Christmas tree. He set it in the window and went straight into the back to find the box of decorations he'd collected over the years. Then he went to his stock and picked out a couple of new baubles that he was selling. Soon, the tree was wrapped with twinkling blue lights and decorated with Star Wars, anime and Lord of the Rings trinkets and baubles. On the top of the tree, he placed a cardboard cutout of the One Ring.

'And in the darkness, bind them,' he murmured as he placed it on the tree. Then he stood back and admired his handywork. 'And now back to work.'

He turned. The shop was empty, but that was to be expected. The school rush hadn't started yet, but it would. He had a number of comic books and graphic novels fresh from the printers, ready and waiting for some teenage regulars.

In the meantime, Matt headed to the back of the shop to fetch some stock to replenish the Christmas decorations he'd plundered from his own shelves. He had to step over his sleeping bag at one point and gave a deep sigh, hands on his hips as he looked down at it.

'I need to make some changes, don't I.'

No one answered.

'Maybe Lilah would rent me her second bed-room.'

Matt couldn't be sure, but it was as if the room went cold. He gave a shiver and a frown, looking around. 'Is that you, Lillian? Or is the door open?'

He hadn't heard the bell go. As far as he was aware, he was still alone in the shop.

'Is that a no about renting Lilah's second bedroom? Fine. Nothing wrong with flatmates, though,' he muttered, kicking the sleeping bag. 'I reckon that's how a lot of people meet these days, you know. In house shares.'

The temperature somehow dropped further, raising goosebumps on his arms beneath his jumper.

'Okay, okay, I'm sorry. I get it. That idea is vetoed.'

The bell ringing brought him back to the real world and to the front of the shop with the last of the stock. He found Stanley lowering into the armchair and taking off his hat.

'Oh good, it's nice and warm in here.' He began unwrapping his scarf and met Matt's eyes. 'Still living here, are you?'

Matt smiled to himself.

'Was it colder in here when I wasn't?' He turned to go put the kettle on.

'Yes!' Stanley called after him.

Matt made Stanley a cup of tea and brought out a plate of biscuits, then made himself a coffee. He sat at his counter, sipping the drink, watching absent-mindedly as Stanley dunked his biscuit into the tea.

'Nice tree,' said Stanley, whipping the biscuit out just before it broke, and taking a bite.

'Thanks. Me and Lilah just went tree shopping.'

'Oh. You and Lilah?'

'Yeah. Well. She's new and she asked where to get a tree from, and...' Matt shrugged.

'And you're after her flat?'

'Oh, no. That's all sorted.'

'But if you struck up a relationship with her, you'd get her flat. In a way.'

Matt blinked at him.

'What?'

'If you were sleeping with her. Keep up. She falls in love with you and asks you to move in. Suddenly you have the flat too. Until she dumps you.'

Matt blinked again. The thought hadn't occurred to him and he couldn't figure out why it hadn't occurred to him.

'You don't think she thinks I'm thinking that, do you?'

It was Stanley's turn to blink at Matt. He stared

back at him.

'What?'

Matt shook the conversation away.

'It's not like that. She's nice and she's my new neighbour. That's all. I went Christmas tree shopping with Lillian once. What's the difference?'

'The difference is that Lillian often mothered you.'

Matt smiled.

'Not always. Sometimes she was like a fun aunt.' His smile fell. 'Probably like she was to Lilah.'

'Hmm. She was special, was Lillian. Always had time for people who needed it. Perhaps your Lilah takes after her. Lillian dragged me out of my shell when my wife died. I needed her, then. Maybe Lilah is going to do the same for you. Pick up where Lillian had to drop off.'

Matt stared down into his coffee. How were they still talking about this?

'What are your Christmas plans?' he tried.

'Hmm.' Stanley took a gulp of his tea. 'Christmas dinner with my sister in London. My nephew is driving me there, picking me up on his way past.'

'Where's he coming from?'

'Cornwall. He works for the council there.'

Matt wondered briefly if Stanley's nephew did anything about the housing situation in Cornwall; they had bigger problems than the little Dorset-coast tourist town Matt and Stanley lived in.

'Nice.'

'My sister is retired now, of course, but she was a nurse in London for a long time. Her husband was a firefighter and then a consultant. They managed to get quite a nice house, considering.'

'Considering it's London?'

'Hmm. I'm quite looking forward to it. It'll be nice to not be alone.' Stanley's eyes lifted to Matt's. 'Are you spending it with family?'

'My parents.' Matt nodded.

'The parents who have a spare bedroom and don't live too far away?'

'On the other side of town.'

'Which isn't far, now, is it? By god, if you think that's far, I think you should take a year to travel the world. That'll open your eyes.'

Matt didn't appreciate the tone, but he didn't say anything. He was well aware of how big the world was and that his parents were basically down the road.

'Lilah moved back in with her parents when she lost her job,' he murmured, mostly to himself.

'Girl knows what's best,' said Stanley pointedly, raising his silver, bushy eyebrows at Matt and drinking the last of his tea. 'There's no shame in it,' he added gently. 'It's not your fault, what's happening with the housing market here. It's the fat cats in London who are at fault. Even if you had a deposit and a mortgage behind you, what person your age who runs a comic book shop in a little town like this can afford the million-pound houses around here?'

'Not all of them are a million pounds,' Matt said, almost out of a habit.

'Most of them are overpriced. That's my point. Do you know lovely Deirdre?'

'No?'

'She owns a little two-bed cottage. It doesn't have a sea view, it's at the bottom of a hill and there's no parking. Well, she's moving north to be closer to her daughter. By my reckoning, that little two-bed cottage should be no more than two hundred thousand, if that. It's quite run down. An investor has offered her double that for it. Bearing in mind it needs a new roof and probably more besides. Four hundred! For two bedrooms! Imagine what Lillian could have got for the flat and this shop. Although Deirdre's cottage is much prettier. It has curb appeal, as they say.'

'So does this place. Maybe not the shop, because it's a shop, but the flat does.'

'Exactly.'

And Lillian had given it all away, likely knowing that Lilah would live in the flat rather than sell it and that Matt would relish the chance of owning his shop.

He stroked his counter affectionately as the option of selling the shop and moving somewhere more affordable vanished from his mind.

'She was so good to us,' he murmured.

'Yes, she was. And she'd be worried sick about

you if she knew you were living here.'

Matt looked up and around the shop, wondering if Lillian was listening to this.

'How do you even start that conversation?' he wondered out loud. 'Hey Mum, hey Dad, your son has failed and has nowhere to live, can I move back in?'

Stanley gave him a look.

'Tell them you were kicked out of your flat because the owner decided to sell to money-grabbers from London, that there's barely anything for long-term rent in this damn town these days, and you're currently sleeping in the back of your very successful shop when you could be paying them rent for your old bedroom.'

'Well, you put it that way...' Matt sighed. 'My very successful shop, huh?'

'Yes. Speaking of which, I overheard a young lad in a coffee shop yesterday talking to his friends about Dungeons and Dragons. I've always wanted to give that a go.'

Matt smiled.

'So does Lilah. I'm near the end of a campaign right now, but I'm starting a new one next month, you and Lilah will get first dibs.'

Stanley grinned.

'Perfect. What are you doing?'

Matt had pulled his phone from his pocket.

'I'm going to call my mum and see if they want to have dinner tonight, so I can tell them what you just said. About renting my old bedroom, not about Dungeons and Dragons.'

'Good.'

Matt found his mother's contact and hit call, holding the phone to his ear.

'Hi,' she answered quickly.

'Tell her I say hi,' Stanley whispered in a whisper that was the same volume as his normal voice.

Matt shot him a look in return, followed by a nod, and then turned away, wandering to the back of the shop as he asked his mother how she was.

'And get some more biscuits!' Stanley called after him.

'Dinner would be wonderful,' Matt's mother said. 'What's the occasion?'

'Erm, celebrating,' said Matt, his mind whirring. 'Lillian leaving me the shop.'

'Yes! You're officially on the property ladder.'

'Yeah...'

'It's a shame you didn't get the flat upstairs.'

'No, well, Lillian decided her niece needed it more, which is fair. She's family. And really nice.' Matt clenched his eyes shut. Why did he keep bringing up how nice Lilah was with everyone?

'Well, that's good. Imagine if you didn't get on? I mean, it's not like you live at the shop, but still. Is the niece out at work during the day?'

'Lilah. She's Lilah. And no, she's not working right now, I guess.'

'Oh. So, she's home all the time? Definitely a

good job you get on. At least you can escape home in the evenings.'

'Yeah... Well, dinner tonight, on me, and—'

'How about the local pub? They always do good food and there's no driving involved.'

'Sure, that'd be great. And—'

'It'll be lovely to see you. It feels like it's been a while, even though you're just down the road. And you'll have to catch me up on Danny and his family, of course. It really feels like everything's turning up, other than the loss of poor Lillian. Doesn't it? Everything's going to be okay.'

Matt rubbed the space between his eyes where a headache was starting to set in.

'Yeah. Yeah. Everything's going to be okay.'

'Did I keep interrupting you? What was it you were going to say?'

'Oh, only... Never mind, I'll see you tonight, yeah?'

'I'll book a table and let you know the time.'

They said their goodbyes and hung up. Matt stayed staring at his blank screen for far too long, until there came a knock behind him. He turned, guessing that Stanley had come looking for him and the biscuits. There was no one there, but down by his feet was a yellow rose petal.

16

At first, Lilah thought the loud crash was Lillian moving something. She opened her eyes to the darkness of the bedroom and listened. Was Lillian trying to tell her something? Was there an emergency?

There came another bang and then a raised voice.

Frowning, Lilah sat up in bed and listened again. The noise was coming from downstairs.

Heart pounding, her mind filled with visions of Matt's shop being broken into, she swung her legs out of bed and grabbed more clothes. She pulled them on as she strode through the dark flat to the living room window and looked down. Expecting to see figures clad in dark clothes, maybe with a brick to smash the shop window, Lilah made an involuntary noise at the sight of Matt fumbling with his keys.

She straightened and shifted from one foot to the other and back again. Was he all right? Should she just go back to bed?

A loud swear word sounded from downstairs and Lilah's frown returned. She watched him for a moment, trying to work out what he was doing. Why was he trying to get into the shop so late? And why was he struggling so much?

It didn't take long for her to realise he was drunk. He dropped his keys for the fourth time, struggled to pick them up and nearly fell backwards into her front door.

Sighing hard, she made her way downstairs, slipped her shoes over her bare feet and pulled on a warm coat. Then she unlocked her front door and opened it.

Matt was sitting just on the other side, staring at his feet and making a low whistling noise.

'What are you doing?' she whispered, aware of all the dark windows looking out at them, presumably hiding neighbours who were hopefully still sleeping.

'Shh!' Matt looked up at her by bending his neck back so he saw her upside down, and put a finger to his lips. 'Shush.'

Lilah crouched so she was almost level with him.

'Matt, what's going on?' she whispered.

'I have to go to bed. Gotta open the shop early,' he slurred, gesturing at the shop. Then he hesitated and stared at the shop's door, before turning to look at the door behind Lilah. 'Is this the right door?'

'No,' Lilah told him. 'You're at your shop. You

need to go home and sleep this off.' She straightened and folded her arms, wondering if he would
make it home in one piece. Maybe she should invite
him upstairs to sleep it off. This wasn't quite how
she'd envisioned inviting Matt upstairs again, plus
she also wanted to get up early in the morning, and
she had a feeling a drunk Matt wouldn't help with
that.

'This is home.'

'What? No. Matt. You need to go where you live.
This is your shop.' Lilah sighed again, glancing up
her stairs, weighing up whether it would be easier
to just get him upstairs and on her sofa. 'I could call
you an Uber? Do they have those here? Or I can give
you a lift. Yes. I'll give you a lift.' She turned and
found her car keys. 'Come on. It won't take long.'

'No, no, no, no,' said Matt, shaking his head.
'S'all right. I am home. C'mon.'

He reached up and pretty much dragged her
down to the ground as he lifted himself to his feet.
She held on to him and then helped steady him.

'Matt. This is your shop.'

'I know!' he yelled.

'Shh!' Lilah admonished, but his loud voice had
made her flinch and twisted her stomach. 'Matt,
why do you need to go in the shop right now?'

'Because I sleep there.'

'You work there,' Lilah corrected.

'And sleep there.'

They stared at each other for a moment. Or, at

least, Lilah stared at Matt and Matt tried to focus on Lilah, blinking far too much and swaying.

'You're living in your shop?' she murmured.

Matt nodded.

'Not for long!' he announced, pointing a finger to the sky. Then he went back to fumbling with his keys.

'You don't have a bed in there, though, right?' Lilah frowned, trying to picture the back of Matt's shop that she'd never seen. For all she knew, he had a whole bedroom, kitchen and ensuite at the back, but knowing the rough size of the building, she doubted it.

'Sleeping bag,' Matt muttered. 'Not for long. Everything's going to be okay.'

Lilah watched him for a moment, then made a decision. Just as the decision was silently made, Matt got his key into the lock and opened his shop door. He shushed the bell above it and staggered inside. Lilah followed him, closing the door behind them. He didn't move to lock it, instead stumbling towards the back, shushing every display cabinet and shelf he bumped into.

She followed him into the back, through a door and into a small room with a tiny kitchenette area and, on the floor, a rolled up sleeping bag and pillow. Matt kicked at it, then dropped to his knees on the sleeping bag. Before he could topple over completely, Lilah let out a loud, 'Nope!' and grabbed his arm.

He looked up at her, bewildered.

'I'm not having this,' she told him. 'Come upstairs. You can sleep on the spare bed. Ridiculous that I have a spare bed and you're down here in a sleeping bag. Why didn't you say anything? Come on.' She heaved on his arm and Matt clumsily stood and let her guide him back out of the shop.

'Lillian said no,' he told her feebly. 'I'm not allowed in the spare room.'

'Well, Lillian isn't here now. It's my spare room now.'

'No, no. Lillian said I mustn't ask you.'

Lilah glanced at Matt and then put a hand out to him.

'Keys, please.'

He gave her his keys and she locked the shop up. Then she guided him gently through her front door where he swayed, looking up at the stairs.

'So many stairs,' he whispered.

'Yeah. Go on, up you go.'

Matt made his way slowly, Lilah right behind him.

'Lillian told you not to ask me about my spare room?'

Matt nodded, and Lilah put out a hand to catch him as he almost missed a step. 'I wonder why she did that,' she mused. 'I really don't mind. All you had to do was say. Maybe not when we first met, but—' Lilah stopped and watched Matt's back. 'Is this why you were so upset about not getting the flat?'

'It'd solved everything,' Matt agreed, reaching the top of the stairs.

Lilah guided him to the bathroom.

'Use the toilet, carefully, and wash your face.'

'M'toothbrush is downstairs.'

'Oh well.'

Lilah closed the door and went into the second bedroom, pausing at the door to look at how much work it needed. Well, those boxes would need moving anyway seeing as her parents were coming to stay.

She started with piling the boxes alongside one wall, clearing space in the room. Once that was done she went into one of the boxes she'd purposefully kept close and dug around until she found a clean sheet, duvet cover and pillowcases. Then she got to work changing the bed.

When she was finished, she realised Matt hadn't reappeared. Her insides fizzing with anxiety, she rushed to the bathroom and gently pushed at the door.

'Matt? Are you decent? Are you all right?'

'Hmph.'

She opened the door and found Matt lying on the bathroom floor, his cheek against the lino.

'It's so nice and cold,' he told her in a squashed voice.

'Great. Well, the bed is clean and nice and probably cold, too.' Lilah held out a hand for him, but Matt only stared at it. 'Please, Matt. Come on. Come to bed.'

He laughed, the noise shocking in the otherwise dark silence.

'I'd love to go to bed with you,' he said into the floor, his eyes closing.

Lilah stopped, her arm still outstretched.

'Well, maybe just come with me right now to this bed and we'll see about the rest when you're not drunk, yeah?'

Matt peered up at her and then nodded, unsticking his face from the floor and groaning as he found his feet with her help.

He plonked onto the freshly made bed and went to lie back.

'Wait!' Lilah rushed out, filled a glass with water in the kitchen and then came back, taking care not to slosh the drink. 'Here. Drink some of this first. It'll help with the hangover.'

'I don't get hangovers.'

'Oh yeah? How old are you?'

'Twenty-one.'

Lilah laughed without thinking and then watched Matt as he took the glass and stared into the water. Gently, she sat beside him on the bed.

'Sip it,' she ordered. He did as he was told. 'Were you out with Danny tonight?'

Matt shook his head, sipping more water.

'My parents.'

'You got this drunk with your parents?'

'I got scared,' he told her in his hushed voice, then he frowned into his drink. 'Stupid, getting scared of talking to your own parents.'

'Why were you scared?'

'Had to ask them if I could move back home. Because I'm a failure.'

Lilah felt that like a knife in her gut.

'Oh,' she managed. 'Matt, you're absolutely not a failure. The shop is doing well, isn't it?'

Matt nodded.

'But I'm homeless.'

'How come?'

He glanced up at her and sniffed back what she realised were tears.

'Landlord kicked me out so some rich guy could buy it and use it as a holiday home. This whole town is just a load of holiday homes. No one who grew up here can afford to live here anymore.'

'Danny lives here?'

'His wife is a doctor and has rich parents. They're gonna outgrow the house soon, though, then they'll be in trouble. 'Xcept her parents will prob'bly bail them out again. And then she'll have the baby and go back to work and earn loads. 'Cause women are magic.'

'Right.' Lilah smiled. 'And there isn't anywhere else to rent?'

Matt shook his head.

'They go so quick. I've tried.' His voice strained, his eyes welling up.

Lilah deflated, moved so he leaned against her and put an arm around his shoulders.

'Sip the water,' she told him.

He did so, his hands trembling a little.

'Bought my parents dinner tonight to ask them if I could move back into my old bedroom. Because I'm a child and a failure—'

'You're not.'

'—and I couldn't even do that right. Couldn't ask them. Too scared. Mum just went on and on and on about how good everything is. Danny's married. Danny has a house. Danny's going to have two children. And isn't it all wonderful. But it isn't wonderful. I don't have a wife or a house or two children. I have a shop filled with toys. That's what my parents call it. A toy shop.' The tears started spilling down Matt's face. 'And now I'm going to own a toy shop and live with my parents. 'Xcept I'm not because I didn't ask them.' He wiped his face with the back of his hand. 'I even failed at that.'

'Oh, Matt.' Lilah left for a moment and returned with a box of tissues, which she passed to him. He cradled the box in his lap before slowly pulling out a tissue. 'You're not a failure. This is just a blip and it's not your fault. You can afford rent, right? It's just there's nowhere *to* rent, and I imagine that puts the rent up everywhere, which means maybe eventually you won't be able to afford it even though business is good.'

'That doesn't help,' Matt murmured before

blowing his nose.

'And how is business good?' Lilah continued. 'This is a tourist town and it should be dead right now. But you're open every day—'

'I live there.'

'—with customers. You're doing really well.' She looked at him as he dried his face. 'You're really good at the community side of it, aren't you. That's what it is. Helping people out, creating a comfortable space, doing the games and events. I bet all the kids know about your shop, and all their geeky parents. Right?'

'Yeah.'

'And Stanley.'

'Yeah, Stanley.'

'You're good at this, Matt. It's not your fault the housing market is a shambles.' Lilah hesitated and looked around the room. 'I'm really sorry Lillian didn't leave you this flat. Maybe she would have if she'd known you were living in the shop. And I'm sorry she told you not to ask me about this room.' Lilah frowned. 'My parents are coming for Christmas, but after that, maybe we can work out a lodging situation...' She trailed off. She probably should give that some thought before she suggested it to Matt, not that he'd likely remember all of this in the morning.

He sniffed.

'Thanks. I'm okay. Everything's going to be all right.' He smiled. 'My mum keeps saying that.'

'You're not a failure,' Lilah reminded him, giving his shoulder a squeeze. They'd never been this close before and, under the heavy scent of alcohol, she could just about smell the everyday Matt. It was good enough to want to curl up on the bed with him.

She did consider it, but was reminded that he could throw up at any moment.

Taking the half-drunk glass of water from him, she placed it on the bedside table and suggested he lie down. Matt didn't need telling twice. He melted backwards, his eyes shut by the time his head hit the pillow. Lilah wondered what to do next and settled on removing his shoes and finding a blanket to throw over him.

Then she returned to the kitchen and came back with a large mixing bowl that had belonged to Lillian.

'Matt? I'm going to leave this here, in case you need to be sick.'

She placed the bowl next to him on the bed and he made a noise as if he'd heard but couldn't open his eyes at that moment. With a small smile, Lilah kissed his forehead and then went back to her own bed, leaving his door ajar, just in case she needed to rush back.

17

There were too many sensations at once, and they all woke Matt up with a start. He groaned before opening his eyes, at both the drumming and just how dry his mouth was. It might as well have had sand in it. In fact – he tried moving his tongue around – maybe it did have sand in it. Did he go to the beach?

No. No, there was no sand. Just the dryness associated with a desert.

Once his tongue was moving, he realised the drumming he could hear was coming from his own head. His whole skull pounded with the beat of his pulse, and each boom made his stomach lurch.

His bladder was also incredibly full, which made moving painful.

Matt groaned again, louder this time, and attempted to open his eyes. His eyelids were stuck together, eyes glued shut. He almost panicked but then managed to wrench them open before immediately closing them against the harsh morning light.

'Wwwhaaa...'

The back room of the shop didn't have a window. Why was there so much light? Had he fallen asleep at the front of the shop? His chest tightened. Could everyone see him?

No, that couldn't be. When he thought about it, he was lying on something soft and comfortable. This wasn't his sleeping bag, and it wasn't the floor.

Matt attempted to open his eyes again and this time, prepared, he blinked furiously until his eyes adjusted. He was in a bedroom, one he didn't recognise.

All of the swear words he knew filled his mind and he sat up, instantly regretting it, crying out and lowering himself back on the bed. His hands clutched his throbbing head and then there came another knocking. It took him a moment to notice this new knocking wasn't coming from inside his skull. He looked at the door in horror, which didn't dissipate when Lilah stuck her head around, her eyes tightly shut.

'I heard a cry. Are you all right? Are you decent?'

Matt looked down at himself.

'Er... mmph.'

'I'll take that as a yes.' Lilah opened her eyes and gave him a kind smile. 'Are you all right?'

Matt nodded and flinched as pain shot through his head. Lilah watched him, nodded and disappeared, closing the door. He waited, wondering if she'd come back. When she didn't, he glanced around the room.

This wasn't her bedroom.

He'd expected relief, but instead there was a hint of sadness about knowing that they probably hadn't slept together. Although, when he gave it more thought, he was glad. That night was a blank.

He sat up as the door opened again and Lilah came in with a glass of water, a plate of buttered toast and a couple of painkillers.

'Here. Take these.' She placed them all on the bedside table nearest Matt.

It was then he noticed the half-drunk glass of water and an empty mixing bowl. He swallowed hard on his dry mouth and took the fresh water from her.

'Sip it,' she ordered just as his lips touched the glass. 'If you gulp, you'll make yourself sick.'

Matt took a few experimental sips, the dryness of his mouth washing away, until his bladder reminded him of its full presence.

'Feel pretty rough, huh?' Lilah was saying.

He nodded and gave her back the glass.

'I, erm...' He checked his body and found himself fully clothed. Relieved, he gestured towards the hall and bathroom.

Lilah frowned in confusion but made space for him to move his legs over the edge of the bed, where he stopped while the world span.

'Uurhh.' He held his head in his hands. 'What happened?'

'I don't know. You tell me.'

'It's a blank.'

Lilah gave a gentle sigh and sat beside him on the bed.

'You came to the shop very drunk, couldn't get your key in, so I came down to help, discovered you've been living in your shop and invited you up here. Nothing happened,' she added quickly. 'You fell asleep pretty much as soon as you hit the bed. And look, you weren't sick!' She grinned, holding up the mixing bowl. The grin slowly faded. 'Oh, are you going to be sick now?'

'No. No, but my bladder's about to explode.'

'Oh! Then go, go, go!' Lilah shifted out of the way, giving Matt a clear run for the bathroom. He wished he could move that fast.

Standing was a start, and he paused to check he had his balance, then he tottered out of the bedroom and into the bathroom, leaning against the wall and the nice cold tile.

When he was finished, he washed his hands and stared at his reflection in the mirror.

This was not how this should have gone.

The night was coming back to him in fits and starts, and his stomach grumbled at the thought of the toast waiting for him on the bedside table. But Lilah was in there, Lilah with her kind eyes and questions.

His eyes were red rimmed, dark marks beneath them. He splashed cold water on his face and took a deep breath before opening the door. Even as he walked to the bedroom, his cheeks were burning.

Lilah was still sitting on the bed. She gave him another smile.

'It's okay,' she told him. 'I'll leave you to it. Don't worry about crumbs. But, look, if you're struggling, there's always this bed if you need it. You don't need to ever sleep downstairs in a sleeping bag.'

The ground fell away from Matt. He could only nod and mumble, 'Thank you.'

When he did nothing else other than stand there, staring at the toast on the bedside table, Lilah stood.

'I'll get you a towel. You can use the shower if you want?'

There was nothing in the world that Matt wanted more in that moment, other than the toast.

He nodded gratefully and collapsed back onto the bed as Lilah passed him, closing the door behind her.

Matt ate the toast, trying to put the memory pieces of last night back together. Lilah popped in and gave him a big, fluffy bath sheet along with some directions for the tricky shower. Once he'd finished eating, he slid quietly into the bathroom and stood under the hot water with his eyes shut, pretending he was anywhere but at this moment in his life.

Matt made a quick exit from Lilah's after the shower, thanking her profusely but claiming he had deodorant and clean clothes downstairs in his shop.

Once changed, he opened the shop and sat behind his counter, staring blankly at his laptop screen. The bell above the door dinged and he looked up to find Lilah walking in carrying two mugs. She passed him one.

'Thought you could probably use a coffee after all that,' she said. 'How's your head?'

'Still sore. Thank you, for the gift from the gods.' He wrapped his hands around the mug and brought it to his nose to fill his head with the scent of the stuff.

'What?' Lilah grinned.

'Oh. Sorry. Ignore me. Don't have enough defences up.'

Lilah gave him a strange look, which was to be expected.

'You don't have to keep up your defences around me. Ever. Just be you.'

That wasn't expected. Matt stared at her.

'Really?'

'Really! You should be yourself.'

'But... people look at me strange when I do that.'

Lilah laughed and the sound shifted the soreness of Matt's head, soothing it a little.

'Good! Let them. So, what are you going to do about last night?'

Matt filled his mouth with coffee before he

answered.

'How much did I let slip?'

'Everything. Well, I don't know if it's everything. You had dinner with your parents so you could ask if you could move back in with them, but they call your shop a toy shop, so you couldn't. Then, somehow you got drunk. Not sure how. I mean, I know how. So, what're we going to do about that?'

'It's "we", now?' Matt almost gave a confused frown, but pain shot through his head, so he worked on keeping his forehead flat.

'I don't know how much you remember,' Lilah started slowly. 'My parents are coming to stay for Christmas, but after that, that bedroom is available should you want to rent it.'

Matt stared down into his coffee.

'I know, I know. Lillian said no. But she has to let go at some point, and that bedroom is mine now. I mean, because it's in my flat. So it's my decision to offer it to you,' Lilah added, a little too quickly.

'Thank you,' Matt said quietly, still staring at the rich murk of his coffee. 'You're my knight in shining armour.'

Lilah grinned, lifting her chin a little higher.

'But I think I need to just be brave and talk to my parents.'

'Okay. I'm sure it'll all be fine,' came Lilah's soft voice.

'Hmm. Yup.'

'Did they see you so drunk?'

'Oh, no. No. They left the pub before me.'

'Right.'

'And I stayed and drank.'

'Okay.'

'And drank and drank.'

'Yeah.'

'And then I came back here because...' Matt clenched his eyes shut for a moment. 'I'm sorry I woke you up. Really. I am sorry. This is so embarrassing,' he added under his breath.

'No, don't be.' She waved any hint of humiliation away with her free hand. 'I get it. I've been there, remember. I mean, I didn't do any of that.'

'No?'

'No, I told my parents I was struggling and asked if I could come back home and they said yes, and I did.'

Matt nodded to himself.

'Yup, sounds about right. I always make things harder than they have to be.'

Lilah laughed and leaned against the counter. Matt was about to point out the empty armchair but Lilah knew it existed and, besides, it would mean her moving away from him to sit. From this distance, he could smell her soft scent; he could reach out to touch her. He didn't, but he could, if she'd wanted.

'Look,' Matt started hesitantly, 'what I said last night...'

'What did you say last night?'

'About...' He sighed. 'I remember it. Sort of. Bits of it. But I felt like such a failure last night. I still do, really. Have done for a while now.'

'Getting kicked out of your flat will do that,' Lilah agreed. 'But just because one part of your life feels like a failure doesn't mean you are one. This is just a blip.'

Matt smiled.

'Yeah.' His smile dropped. 'It's just I've always been like this. A bit of a failure.'

Lilah gave a soft chuckle.

'Show me a nice person who hasn't.'

That stumped Matt and he stared into his coffee, trying to think of someone.

'Danny?'

'Nah. He's just not telling you about it.'

'Ha. Yeah, now that you mention it.'

'So, when are you going to call your parents?' Lilah asked.

Matt shrugged.

'Now? I guess. Get it over with. I mean, I'll pay them rent. It's not that I can't afford a place, it's just there's no places to rent. And I'll keep looking. I did think about converting the back of the shop, but...'

'It's not big enough,' Lilah finished for him. She watched him carefully for a moment and he narrowed his eyes, reading her mind. When she opened her mouth to speak, he got there first.

'No.'

'You didn't let me—'

'Nope.'

'But you don't know what I was going to say.'

'You were going to offer me your spare room again.'

'Well... yeah. The commute would be good.' Lilah flashed Matt a smile that made him glad he was sitting down.

'Thanks for the offer, but I think Lillian's right. It wouldn't work.'

'Oh.' Lilah's expression fell and Matt fought the instinct to dive across the counter to wrap his arms around her. 'Why not?'

Matt gathered himself. One little hangover and suddenly all these thoughts started coming out.

'I don't know. But Lillian was insistent.'

Lilah accepted this, sipping her coffee.

'Speaking of which, I'm going to the gallery you showed me today, to see if they have any of her artwork. I wonder what they'll do with it when they're done. Maybe I can get it back. Or maybe there won't be any. Either way, let me know if you fancy joining me. I'd love the company.'

Matt nodded automatically, then the thoughts came racing back. Was she asking him out? No, it was a friendly invitation. That was all. Maybe he should have made that hot shower a cold one.

'Sounds good. If you go when I'm free, I'll come.'

'Great! Also, I wasn't expecting my parents to come here for Christmas. They're coming to celebrate Lillian. Which is lovely, of course, but the flat is a state. And I haven't even started Christmas shopping yet. I noticed signs for a Christmas market the other day, and Bea mentioned she has a stall there. She and Lillian used to have a stall together...' Lilah drifted off into thought, then snapped back. 'Have you done your Christmas shopping?'

'You know, I sell great Christmas presents.' Matt waved his arm across his shop.

Lilah looked around and made a strained noise.

'You do. You do. But I sort of want my parents to make happy noises when they unwrap presents, not confused, pretend-happy noises.'

Matt laughed despite himself.

'You wouldn't be shocked at how many people say that about this place.'

Lilah grinned and gave him a look.

'They're just not your target audience. Come on. This place does great.'

'Yeah. Oh, Stanley's down for the next DnD campaign, too. If you're still up for that? I need to start getting a list together.'

'Absolutely! Right, I'm going to the beach with Lillian's paints to meet Bea. When are you free for a walk to the gallery?'

Matt shrugged.

'Two-ish?'

'I will see you at two-ish. Don't worry about the mug, I'll get it back next time I see you. Go call your parents before you think too much more about it.'

Lilah gave Matt an awkward little wave and left the shop before slipping through her front door. Matt watched her go, a smile plastered on his face, and as she went his headache tiptoed back. He drank the last of his coffee while it was still hot, staring at his phone. Once the mug was empty, he hit his parents' number and held the phone to his ear, biting his lip until his mother answered.

18

At quarter past two, Lilah and Matt walked to the gallery against the wind.

'How did the chat with your parents go?' Lilah shouted over her shoulder.

'Good,' came the response. 'Well, it went okay. As well as I expected, I guess.'

'So... not good?'

'No, it's fine. They said I could move back in for as long as I need.'

'That's great!'

Lilah glanced back to Matt when he didn't respond, wondering if his words had gotten lost in the wind. He was busy looking down at the pavement as he walked, his shoulders hunched up to his ears. 'Are you sure you're okay to close? What if someone comes in?'

'Nah,' said Matt as they turned a corner and the old mill and gallery revealed themselves. The sky was a pale blue, the wind having seemingly blown the clouds away, and for once, everything was calm and crisp. 'I left a note on the door. It'll be fine. And look, the gallery's open.'

They walked inside and were met with white walls decorated with framed artwork and canvasses at regular intervals down the long building, leading onto square rooms that were much the same. A counter with a woman behind was over to the right, and she smiled as they walked in. It was so light and quiet, Matt looked up at the lighting and large windows, while Lilah walked over to the woman behind the counter.

'Hi, erm, hello. I was wondering if you have any artwork by Lillian Chancery?'

'Hi. Yes, we do, just over here. Are you a fan?' The woman moved from the counter and led Lilah towards a back room.

Lilah glanced over her shoulder to Matt. He noticed her moving away and jogged to catch up.

'Actually, I'm her niece. She sort of kept the extent of her art secret, for some reason. I've uncovered some pieces at her flat and then Matt, here, told me she might have some work up here.'

'I wonder why she kept it secret,' the woman mused, stopping in front of a collection of paintings and smiling up at them.

Matt's eyes widened and then he did a strange reverse snort laugh. Lilah didn't blame him. She stared at the paintings, the largest of which appeared to be an oil painting of Stanley completely naked.

'Oh.'

Matt had put a hand over his mouth and widened his eyes further when Lilah looked to him.

The smaller paintings were mostly of close ups of Stanley's naked body, except for one beachscape. Lilah blinked and put her focus on the beach.

'Does Stanley know about this?' she whispered to Matt.

He shrugged, his shoulders shaking with the effort of not laughing. She turned back to the woman.

'How long does the art stay here for?'

'Until New Year, unless sold.'

'Sold!' croaked Matt.

'Right. And then what happens?'

She gave Lilah a strange look.

'Then Ms Chancery will come and collect whatever hasn't sold.'

Lilah stared at her until she realised the woman was becoming uncomfortable. Without looking, she tapped Matt's arm with the back of her hand, telling him off. He cleared his throat and tried to get a grip.

'My aunt passed away earlier this year.'

The woman's expression fell.

'Oh! I'm so sorry. I didn't know. I'm so sorry for your loss.' She turned to look at the paintings. 'That's such a shame. How—' she started.

'Could I pick them up in the new year?' Lilah interrupted, knowing what question was coming. 'If I bring paperwork to prove who I am and stuff?'

The woman's lips twitched.

'We would need Ms Chancery's consent,' she said with a grimace.

'How about a death certificate and evidence of next of kin?'

She nodded.

'Yes, that would do it. Again, I'm so sorry.'

Lilah smiled.

'Thanks. It's okay. She was ill for a long time, but she hid it well.' Lilah looked back up to the paintings. 'Do you know if she had art in any other galleries?'

'No. Not to my knowledge,' said the woman, crossing her arms and joining Lilah in looking up at naked Stanley. 'I'll leave you to it. Let me know if I can help at all.'

'Thank you. Oh! Has she sold any?'

'Yes. A few of the smaller pieces.'

'That's great.' Lilah turned back to the paintings. 'Thank you.'

'Wonder if any of those were of Stanley,' Matt murmured, sidling closer to Lilah now that they were alone.

'I need to ask whether Lillian was paid for those sales,' Lilah sighed. 'Do you think Lillian and Stanley were...? Is Stanley married?'

'Widowed.'

They stared up at the paintings in silence for a moment.

'Will you ask Stanley about them, make sure he

knows they're here?' Lilah asked, trying to work out if she'd missed anything that meant Lillian's legacy would be missing a vital piece.

'Sure. You know, they're actually really good. Once you get past the whole it's Stanley naked thing.'

Lilah tilted her head at the largest of the paintings.

'They're beautiful,' she murmured.

'What're you going to do with that big one in the new year?'

'Probably ask if Stanley wants it. It should be pride of place somewhere. Maybe over his bed.'

Matt laughed and then slapped a hand over his mouth as it echoed through the gallery.

Once they'd chatted more to the woman working at the gallery, they headed to the café next door and picked up takeaway coffees and muffins, which they ate on their way to the Christmas market in the town hall down the road.

'I haven't been in here before,' Lilah murmured, although she hardly needed to keep her voice down. The place was a bustle of activity. The exact opposite of the gallery.

People of all ages were coming and going, talking loud to be heard over the brass band playing Christmas songs in the corner. All around the hall were stalls selling baked goods, jewellery, artwork, crafts, knick-knacks and a woman reading tarot cards. Lilah was almost tempted to buy a reading until she recognised some art prints just beyond the tarot reader.

'Bea!' Lilah headed straight for the stall, losing Matt on the way.

'Lilah! How lovely that you made it.'

'Oh, I didn't think to buy you a coffee. I'm so sorry. How's it going? Can I help at all?'

'No need, no need, but thank you for thinking of it at all. My husband's around here somewhere, we're taking it in turns. Maybe next year we can have a stall together, once you're feeling more confident and have time to prepare?'

'I'd love that!' Lilah gazed at the art prints on Bea's stall, along with some originals and specifically designed Christmas cards. 'These are all amazing.' Each picture captured an essence of the town, from the gardens and architecture to the esplanade, beach and waves. There was even a colourful print of the beach huts lined up on a sunny day. 'I want to buy them all.'

Lilah's flat was filling with Lillian's artwork as she uncovered pieces. It would be nice, she decided, to have more of Bea's.

'How's the Christmas shopping going?' Bea asked as Lilah tried to choose between prints.

'Great. So far I'm buying these for me and I have nothing for my family. I've got my parents coming for Christmas, so I need to get some things. These are a good start.' She handed the three prints she'd chosen to Bea. 'Two for me, one for Mum. One down, at least one more to go, not including everyone else.'

Bea laughed and slid the prints into a paper bag with a logo she'd designed herself printed in the middle. Lilah paid and then glanced behind her, looking for Matt.

'Will I see you again before Christmas?' she asked as Bea passed her the bagged prints.

'Of course. I'll be in my usual spot right up until Christmas. The kids are coming to us this year, so no need to pack or travel or any of that rubbish. Just need to give the house a quick clean before they arrive, make up beds and make sure we have enough food. Which is always the stressful part. I'll need the painting time to unwind. And coffee and mince pies, if you're up for that?'

'Always!' Lilah grinned. Matt appeared beside her and he made an appreciative noise at the art on Bea's stall. 'I'll see you then. Any luck finding presents?' she asked Matt.

He shook his head and looked up at Bea beaming.

'These are great,' he told her. 'Did you know Lillian painted Stanley nude?'

Bea burst out laughing.

'You finally found that out, huh? How? Did he break and tell you?'

'The paintings are up in the gallery,' Matt told

her.

Bea gasped.

'She never told me. Crafty fox that she was. I'll have to go check them out.'

'Do you think Stanley knows?' Lilah asked.

Bea shook her head.

'Maybe. Perhaps. But I'd let him know if I were you. If only to see the look on his face if he doesn't.'

Matt laughed.

'Can't wait.'

They spent an hour at the market, buying some small items to give as presents, all of which Lilah put into the paper bag containing Bea's prints, making sure she showed everyone she passed Bea's art logo on the bag. After buying another coffee each, and another two for Bea and her husband, they delivered the coffees and left the market, finding a bench on the esplanade, looking out to sea. The waves were smaller today, matching the sunny, crisp weather. Still, there was an icy chill in the air and Lilah wrapped her gloved hands around her coffee cup.

'This was really fun. Thanks for coming with me.'

'Thanks for getting me out of the empty shop,' said Matt, sipping his coffee.

'You've made most things here fun,' Lilah mused.

'Except for when I haven't?'

Lilah smiled and gave Matt a sideways look.

'Oh, I don't know. I didn't mind drunk Matt. He would have been funny if I hadn't been worried about him.'

Matt pulled a face.

'Yeah, sorry about that.'

'I'm not a fan of angry, doesn't-like-me Matt, though.' Lilah gave Matt a light, playful dig with her elbow.

He laughed.

'Me neither, if I'm honest. But if that Matt knew what I know now.'

'What do you know now?' she asked, turning to face him.

He searched her eyes and for a moment everything else fell away, leaving just him in front of her.

'How nice you are,' he said, glancing down to her lips. 'How fun you are.'

'That Lillian wrote you a letter?' Lilah murmured, smiling, watching his mouth.

'And that.' Matt grinned, leaning closer.

'Well, you're nice and fun, too.' Lilah pulled a face at herself. 'I'm so sorry, that was awful.'

Matt laughed again and then a silence fell over them as they watched each other, leaning imperceptibly closer.

'I'm glad that if I couldn't have the flat, that you got it,' Matt murmured.

They were going to kiss. It occurred as a spark in Lilah's mind and her insides flipped pleasurably.

She leaned in, wondering if she could kiss him first.

Matt smiled, then he moved forward and their lips met. He was so warm against the cold that Lilah briefly considered squashing her cold face against his, but that urge was quickly overwhelmed by the tenderness of him kissing her. Their hands were preoccupied with holding their drinks so they didn't spill, and a chilly breeze seemed to force them apart. Matt sat back, watching her. Lilah stayed put, smiling at him.

'Been a while since I did that.'

'Since you kissed a woman by the sea?' Lilah's voice came out huskier than usual and Matt's eyes seemed to flicker.

'Since I kissed a woman.' Matt stopped. 'Probably shouldn't have said that.'

Lilah grinned.

'It's okay. It's been a while for me, too.' She still hadn't sat back. She wanted more, and wondered how she could get Matt to lean in again.

Before she could figure it out, Matt checked the time and the moment wafted away.

'Best get back to the shop.'

A little disappointed, but still mentally spinning from the kiss, Lilah nodded and stood up.

'Let's go.'

19

They didn't talk about the kiss, but Matt replayed it over and over. Especially that afternoon, as he packed up his things in the back room. He couldn't get over the feel of Lilah's lips, her warmth against his chill, her softness, the smell of her. The thought that she was just upstairs was almost too much. He could knock on her front door, see if she invited him in. Maybe they would kiss again, maybe it would lead to more.

Matt was smiling to himself, whistling, as he quickly packed and rolled up his sleeping bag. Most of his belongings were in storage and they would stay there; he didn't want to burden his parents. He just needed a bed and a hot shower, that was all.

His mind took that opportunity to mix the ideas, resulting in picturing Lilah in a hot shower, him stepping inside, wrapping hands around her naked waist.

The bell above the door rang and Matt happily whistled his way to the front of the shop.

There was no one there.

He checked every part of the shop, in case he'd missed someone, and then laughed.

'Don't tell me you can read my thoughts, Lillian,' he told the empty room. 'That's too far. I'm allowed my thoughts. Also, your niece is hot. Who knew.'

The bell rang again and he span round to watch a family of two parents and their two children walk in. Cheeks flushing, Matt grinned and waved awkwardly. 'Hi! Welcome. Let me know if you need help with anything.' He almost ran to the counter and hid behind it while the family mooched around. They bought some small items, were polite and left, leaving Matt hopeful that maybe they hadn't heard.

He closed the shop at half five, backpack swung over his shoulder, rolled up sleeping bag under his arm, and set off into the night. His parents lived just too far away to walk and while Matt could drive, he'd never had much need for a car. Lilah had offered him a ride, but it seemed too soon after kissing her to let her see his parents' house. Especially if it meant they might meet.

Anyway, Danny had offered before her and Matt had accepted. He was waiting in his car further down the road where it was safe to park. Matt opened the door, chucked his stuff in the back, fell into the passenger seat and said, 'I kissed Lilah.'

Danny slowly turned to stare at his friend and for

the longest moment they sat in silence, Matt grinning ear to ear at Danny.

'Did she kiss you back?'

'Yup.'

'Did you do anything else?'

'Nope. To be fair, we were sitting on a bench by the beach and holding coffee cups.'

Danny laughed and clapped Matt on the shoulder.

'Mate! I'm so proud of you.'

'You're *proud* of me for kissing her?'

'I don't think you're remembering how less than two weeks ago you were furious at this woman for taking your flat and effectively making you homeless. I was worried you might never get on, that it'd ruin everything you've built. Now you're kissing! This is huge.'

'It is,' said Matt, a little uncertainly. 'I guess we have come quite far.'

'You have. Although, I don't think Lilah ever had a problem with you.'

'No, I guess, but—'

'Maybe Lillian knew this would happen,' Danny added quietly, pulling out onto the road and heading towards Matt's parents' house.

'Maybe. Hey, did you know she did, erm, what's it called...' Matt sat quietly for a moment, desperately trying to think of the term Bea had reminded him of that morning. 'When you paint naked people.'

'I think it's called painting naked people. Painting nudes?'

'Life drawing! Anyway, she painted a naked Stanley.'

'What?'

'And the paintings are up in the mill gallery.'

'Shut up. Why didn't she tell you?'

'Probably because she knew this is how I'd react.' Matt grinned.

'When did you find this out?'

'This morning. Lilah invited me to the gallery with her because I mentioned Lillian had said something about her art being displayed there. Then we went to the Christmas market. Then we kissed.'

'Quite the day you've been having.'

'Best day ever. It's not going to finish that way, but you can't have everything.'

'I mean, it's going to finish with you in a bed instead of a sleeping bag.'

'Hmm.'

Danny gave Matt a sideways look.

'But it's not Lilah's bed?'

Matt went back to grinning and Danny laughed.

'So, you're going to ask her out? Like, on a date?'

'Is that still what people do?'

Danny frowned.

'How else do you spend time together getting to know each other?'

'I don't know. I just thought they'd have figured

out a better way by now.'

'Well, you could always bring her to our Friends' Christmas Dinner.'

'You're doing that again?'

'Why wouldn't we?'

Matt gave this some thought. Every year Danny and his wife held a Christmas dinner party that was just for friends, and every year Matt went, out of respect for how long he and Danny had been friends. Most years he went alone, and for the last four years he'd ended up filling the fun uncle role with Rosie to avoid actually being alone. It wasn't that the others didn't include him, it was just that conversation inevitably turned to family and relationships and children.

'Hmm. I'm not sure I want to expose Lilah to talk from happily married couples with children. Seems a bit... premature.'

Danny gave a little splutter.

'What're you talking about? Everyone will love to meet her. And if you come together, it could be a first date, and they'd only ask what she does for a living—'

'Nothing, she lost her job.'

'—and why she moved here—'

'Her aunt died.'

'—and if you two are – okay, I get it.' Danny sighed. 'Still, you're both invited.'

'Thanks. I appreciate that.'

Danny pulled up outside Matt's parents' house.

Matt gathered his things, got out and bent down to look at Danny.

'Thanks, mate. I owe you one.'

'Nah, you don't. Remember, both you and Lilah are invited to our Friends' Christmas Dinner. See you for the quiz.'

'Cheers! See you then.'

Matt closed the door and turned to face his parents' house. Behind him, Danny drove away, leaving him standing alone on the pavement with his bags. Steadying himself, taking a deep breath, Matt whispered under his breath, 'Here we go.'

His parents lived in a small end terrace house with a little gate leading to a front path. To the side was a garage and his parents' car sat in the dark on the driveway. There was a light on in the front room window, but the curtains were shut. Christmas hadn't touched the house since he turned sixteen. Matt pushed through the gate, as he had done so many times throughout his life, and took another moment to himself at the front door. Then he knocked twice.

His mother answered.

'Don't you have a key?'

'Yeah, but I didn't want to barge in.'

She shrugged and let him in.

'You know where your bedroom is. Come down when you're ready. Have you eaten?'

'Not yet.'

'I left a piece of cottage pie for you in the oven to

keep it warm.' She made her way back into the living room.

'Thanks, Mum.'

Matt watched her go, then glanced around the hallway. The carpet was burgundy and almost threadbare, it had been there since he was a kid. In front of him was the doorway to the kitchen and off to the left was the living room. To the right, the stairs led up to the three bedrooms. The smallest bedroom, now used for storage, had once belonged to his younger brother, who now lived in Sweden with his husband and stepchildren, and a few months after Matt had moved out, his mother had turned his bedroom into a neutral guestroom. He carried his bags upstairs and threw them on a floor he recognised. The walls may have been painted beige and the curtains and furniture replaced, but the carpet was still the same. Somewhere underneath the impeccably made double bed was a stain from when he'd dropped a bowl of pasta aged fourteen.

It was strange to be in a room with so many memories, that looked nothing like the room he'd grown up in. He sat on the foot of the bed and listened to the muffled sounds of the TV downstairs.

'Home sweet home,' he told the room, already missing Lillian's presence and the smell of his shop.

After making his way downstairs, he popped into the living room to say hi to his dad, then ventured into the kitchen and helped himself to the cottage pie his mum had prepared for him. He ate it sitting on the two-seater sofa in the living room, while his parents took up the three-seater against the other wall. They were watching some sort of crime drama and at first his mother tried to explain what was going on, until she became a bit lost with it all and his father tried to correct her, getting it equally wrong. A silence fell as they went back to watching it.

Matt didn't say anything. It wasn't his place, but also, he had no idea what was going on and didn't really care. The cottage pie was nice and he told his mother so. She gave him a warm smile.

'Miss your cooking,' he told her, filling his mouth.

'You look like you do,' she agreed.

His father sighed.

'No idea what's going on,' he muttered. 'Pretty sure that guy did it, though. The cleaner.'

'That's not the cleaner, he's the professor,' said Matt's mother.

'Oh. Yeah, him.'

Matt's mother started watching him eat, and he attempted to ignore her without much success.

'Have you talked much to Lillian's niece? The one who got the flat instead of you?'

'Erm, yeah...'

'What's her name again?'

'Lilah.'

'I thought it was a two-bed flat,' said his father, still watching the TV, not wanting to miss the reveal of the murderer.

'It is,' said Matt.

'You couldn't rent her second bedroom?' his father asked.

'No.'

'Why not?' asked his mother.

Matt cleaned his plate, his fullness turning a little to nausea.

'Because...' What could he say? He could hardly tell them Lillian's ghost told him he shouldn't. Just as he couldn't tell them that moving in might ruin any chance of a romantic relationship with Lilah.

'Because? Seems like an excellent solution to me. She could probably use the money from your rent, too. What does she do?' his mother asked.

'She just lost her job before she moved here.'

'So, she's unemployed?'

'She's trying to start an art career.'

His mother pulled a face, and a sickening pang of recognition filled Matt's bones. Every part of him wanted to leave. The bed upstairs was nice but, in that moment, he just wanted his sleeping bag on the floor of his shop. His shop that his mother had pulled exactly the same face about.

'That means she definitely needs the money,' said his father, oblivious.

'She's finding her feet and mourning her aunt. She doesn't want me there.'

'But maybe she will, soon. You should ask her,' said his mother.

He nodded in an attempt to end the conversation.

'How was your day?' he tried.

'The usual,' said his mother. 'Christmas is everywhere. It's driving me mad. I'll be glad when it's all over. Can't move for people out there.'

'Well, it is Saturday and the Christmas market was on today.'

'Hmm.'

They sat in silence for a while, the TV loud as they waited to see if Matt's father was right about the murderer.

'I went to the Christmas market,' Matt said, mostly to himself. 'It was nice. I saw Bea, Lillian's artist friend. Lilah's going to take Lillian's place at her stall next year.'

He looked up and found his mother staring at him blankly. 'And the shop is going well,' he added. 'Lilah and Stanley are signed up for the next DnD campaign.'

Her expression became blanker, which he had thought impossible.

'What's that?' she asked.

'Erm, Dungeons and Dragons.'

'The game he used to play with Danny and the boys,' said his father, not taking his attention from the TV.

'Oh, yes.' His mother turned back to the TV.

Matt swallowed hard and silently stood to take his plate and fork back into the kitchen.

'Stick the kettle on,' his mother called.

He did as he was told and made three cups of tea. Sipping his in silence, they discovered that the professor did indeed commit the murder and Matt's father smacked his thigh in vindication. Matt made his excuse and went up to bed. The sheets were clean but the room didn't smell right. It was like being in a weird bed and breakfast, one that made him feel small rather than relaxed. He got into bed, turned off the light and stared up the ceiling. In a desperate attempt to feel better and not miss his shop, he tried to remember what had happened that day.

He'd almost forgotten the kiss!

Matt closed his eyes and went back to it, focusing on Lilah's warm lips until he drifted to sleep and into troubled dreams.

20

Despite the fact that Matt's shop was open at the usual times, Lilah was missing him. She might not have known he was just downstairs during the night all that time, but she was beginning to wonder if she'd sensed his presence somehow. The first night he'd moved into his parents, she'd lain in bed thinking about their kiss that day and feeling horribly alone. As alone as she'd ever felt. In the end, she'd wrapped a blanket around herself on the sofa and talked to Lillian, who had barely responded other than the odd flickering light.

That first morning, waking and knowing Matt wasn't below her, she showered, dressed and waited for him. The moment she heard the shop's door open, she rushed to the kitchen and then made her way carefully downstairs with two mugs of coffee.

'Morning!' She pushed through the door, the bell above her ringing her arrival.

'Hey!' Matt came forward and took his mug from

her. 'Want some biscuits? I've just bought some new packets in case Stanley comes in. I've got gingerbread.' He vanished into the back of the shop before Lilah could respond, so she gave Stanley's armchair an affectionate smile, trying to force the images of his painted naked body from her mind.

'Did you tell Stanley? About the paintings?' she asked when Matt returned.

'Not yet.' He flashed her a playful grin that made her stomach flip.

They leaned on either side of the counter, Matt dipping his gingerbread biscuit into his coffee.

'How was last night?' Lilah asked.

'Awful. But it was nice to be in a bed again. I guess.'

'Is it really that bad? Being back with your parents?'

Matt swallowed his biscuit.

'Let me put it this way: do you get on with your parents?'

'Yeah.'

'Are you friends?'

'Yes.'

'Do they support your decision to move here and not immediately look for a job?'

'Yeah,' said Lilah slowly. 'My dad offered me money, even though I told him I have savings, and my mum told me to give this art thing a serious go. That Lillian would be proud. Even my sister said she'd buy my first painting if it didn't get snapped up.'

Matt looked up at her.

'You have a sister?'

'Yeah. Haven't I mentioned her?'

'You said your parents were coming for Christmas. You never mentioned a sister.'

'Oh.' Lilah waved him away. 'She's married and lives in Italy. They take it in turns, they're with his family this year. She'll come visit next year, I'm sure. And by that point, I need to be good enough to try selling some art.' Lilah frowned. That was the first time she'd put that pressure into words, out loud, and all it did was add more pressure to her shoulders.

'Easy,' said Matt, watching her. 'You're already good enough.'

Lilah scoffed and watched him choose another biscuit.

'Your parents don't support you?'

'Not really. They think this is all a stupid children's hobby, something I'll grow out of, and then I'll regret giving up my old job. You mark their words.' Matt pointed his biscuit at Lilah, then shoved the whole thing in his mouth.

She gave a small laugh.

'I'm sorry.'

He shrugged, his gaze slowly moving back up to meet hers as he chewed and swallowed.

'So, erm, yesterday, huh...' he started.

'You did have quite a day yesterday.'

'Yeah. But the, erm, afternoon...'

They stared at one another and Lilah willed him to finish that sentence. Soon, they were both staring at one another's lips and Matt seemed about to say something when the bell rang and a group of teenagers walked into the shop.

The next night and day passed in a similar fashion, with Lilah venturing to bed later and later, chatting away to Lillian until she began to wonder if her aunt's spirit had gone. Pushed out of her home by her niece's incessant chatter. It meant Lilah wasn't getting up as early and her painting was starting to suffer for it. She met with Bea that morning in a rush, twenty minutes late and full of apologies. When she tried to explain, she stumbled. *Sorry I'm late, the man who was living in his shop downstairs isn't there anymore, but only at night, and I miss him despite spending the mornings chatting over coffee.*

She couldn't say that, so she mumbled something about oversleeping, which was entirely true, and promised it wouldn't happen again. They painted, talked, had coffee and cake, and Lilah returned home and hovered outside her front door, watching Matt through the shop window as he chatted to a couple of customers. The more she secretly watched him through the shop window, the cuter he seemed to get. Some would say he needed a haircut, but Lilah liked how floppy his brown hair had become, especially at the front, meaning he had to keep sweeping it back. It didn't take much for her to start wondering how it would feel to push her fingers through it, to push it back for him before kissing him.

He glanced up at her and smiled, gave her a little wave, and she panicked, waved back and practically walked into her closed front door. As she took a moment to recover, her heart pounding with the sheer adrenaline of embarrassment, Matt opened his shop door and peered around.

'You okay?'

'Hmm.' Lilah nodded.

'Do you want to go to the charity Christmas quiz with me tonight? I'm not going home first so I'll shut up the shop and knock for you, if you fancy?'

Lilah fancied him, but she didn't say that. She only nodded again.

'Hmm. Yup. Okay.'

'Okay. See you then.' Matt shut the door and vanished back into his shop to his customers.

She watched him go and sighed, before finding her keys and letting herself into the flat.

The quiz was four hours away, so she went through more of Lillian's things – a couple of sketchbooks, some clothes and a box of pretty jewellery – then did some drawing, trying to copy one of Lillian's pieces, had a quick bite to eat and showered. She'd just put on a pair of ruby earrings she'd found in Lillian's jewellery box, telling herself they couldn't possibly be real rubies, when Matt knocked on the door. Lilah practically skipped down the stairs before taking a moment to steady herself. She couldn't behave like a normal, rational person if she was skipping around to the beat of her heart, hoping Matt would kiss her again, resisting the urge to jump on him and kiss him herself.

Matt smiled when she opened the door. He hadn't showered, as there wasn't one in the shop, and he was wearing the same clothes he'd been wearing all day, but the sight of his dark eyes and bright smile was enough.

'Ready?' he asked, turning away.

Lilah's heart slowed a little in disappointment.

'Oh. Yeah, sure.' She grabbed her coat and bag, pulled on some flat shoes and stepped out into the cold, dark evening. 'At least it's not raining,' she said as she locked the door and caught up with Matt.

They walked side by side through the town, beneath twinkling fairy lights with the crashing waves as background noise, chatting about their days. The pub's noise reached them before they reached the pub, and Lilah's insides tingled with the thought of being in the warmth, surrounded by so many people.

Matt pushed through the door and the warmth, smell and sheer loudness of the place hit her like a wall. Her step hesitated, but she hurriedly pushed through it and followed Matt through the crowds to the right side of the bar. She was so busy looking down at her feet so she didn't trip, or up at Matt so she didn't lose him, that she didn't have a chance to take in the pub.

'Matt! Lilah! You made it.' Danny appeared with arms somehow outstretched in such a crowded place.

''Course we did,' said Matt, reaching past Danny and hugging a beautiful and heavily pregnant woman standing behind him. 'Lilah, this is Nat, Danny's missus. This is Lilah, who lives in the flat above the shop.'

Lilah plastered a smile on her face and said hello to Nat as her stomach plummeted. The woman who lives in the flat above the shop. That was all?

'What would you like?' Danny asked Lilah.

'Huh?'

'To drink?'

'Oh, erm, just a lemonade for me.'

'Really? You're sure?'

'Yeah. That's fine. I want to keep a clear head for the quiz.'

Danny laughed and then studied her seriously for a moment.

'How about a fancy lemonade? They do raspberry lemonade? Nat has it a lot. It's her pregnancy drink.'

'Sounds good.'

When Lilah turned back to Nat and Matt, only

realising then that their names rhymed, she found them huddled together at a table for four. So much for the date vibes she'd been hoping for.

Danny appeared behind her and passed her a chilled glass of raspberry lemonade and a pint of Guinness, gesturing to the table.

'That's Matt's. Go take a seat.'

'Okay. Thanks.'

Lilah did as she was told, taking the empty seat next to Matt and desperately trying to work out what they were talking about. She didn't need to try for long. The conversation seemed to end as she sat.

'Lilah, how you finding living here? I hope Matt's been showing you around?' asked Nat.

'Oh, yeah. It's great. I love it here,' said Lilah, sipping her drink and watching Matt take a slug of his pint, wiping the foam from his lips.

Danny reappeared, taking the last empty chair between Lilah and Nat and passing his wife her raspberry lemonade.

'I'll hate this in a few weeks,' she told Lilah cheerily, holding up her glass so they could clink their lemonades.

Lilah gave a laugh.

'Is that when you're due?'

'Yeah. I can't wait to not have this huge belly anymore, but then I'll have a buggy and a bag full of nappies and a screaming baby, plus a four-year-old! But at least I'll be able to put all of it down and pick things up from the floor again.'

Lilah didn't know what to say to that so she nodded, made an understanding exhausted face and grinned as best she could before covering it all up with a gulp of lemonade.

A man came round and gave them an answer sheet and a pen.

'What's our team name?' Danny asked the table.

Nat and Matt glanced at one another and Lilah sat back, watching them have a seemingly silent chat.

'The Four Amigos?' Danny offered.

'No!' cried Nat.

'There were only three amigos,' Matt told him. 'There were four ghostbusters.'

'Ghostbusters!' cried Nat.

'We can't be the Ghostbusters. That's stupid. Anyway, it should be something Christmassy.'

'The Four Nutcrackers,' said Lilah without thinking.

Matt stared at her and then he and Nat burst out laughing.

'Put that!' Nat demanded of her husband, pointing at the sheet.

He did so, laughing and shaking his head.

'How long have you known each other?' Lilah finally asked.

'Years,' Nat told her. 'I met Danny at university, when I was twenty. And a few weeks later he introduced me to Matty. So, over ten years.' Her face crumpled as she tried to do maths.

Lilah was stuck on 'Matty', glancing at Matt, desperate for that closeness. Then her world collapsed around her as he met her gaze and gave her a wink, bringing his pint to his lips.

'How's your Christmas trivia?' Danny asked her, forcing Lilah to recover quickly.

'Oh, erm, not good?'

They laughed and Lilah laughed with them, relaxing a little. As the quiz master picked up his microphone and brought the pub to a gentle quiet, introducing himself and the charitable cause of the quiz and the youth football team, Matt sat up straighter and pulled his chair in, closer to Lilah.

Soon they were huddled around the table, Matt and Lilah's elbows up against one another as they softly argued and laughed about possible answers to questions.

'Didn't think you'd be allowed to do this quiz,' Lilah mentioned to Danny during a break, while Matt was at the bar getting in another round. 'As you're involved in the football team.'

'Nah. I didn't organise this, so I'm allowed. And if we win, I'll give the prize to you and Matty to fight over.'

A warm glow grew in Lilah's stomach, stretching out to her fingers.

'What's the prize?'

'First prize is a weekend away, would you believe? Nowhere special, but still. One of the other parents owns a holiday cottage, so it's a weekend there. Second prize is a gift card to a local spa.'

'I reckon you and Matty could share either of those,' said Nat, giving Lilah a knowing look.

Lilah looked away as she agreed, her cheeks burning and she couldn't blame it on the alcohol. Matt rejoined them with drinks just as the second half of the quiz got underway.

Afterwards, as they waited for the points to be counted up, Lilah leaned closer to Danny.

'Did it ever bother you that Nat rhymes with Matt?'

Danny burst out laughing, repeating what Lilah had asked to the others. Matt grinned at Lilah and, under the table, reached out to brush his hand over her fingers resting in her lap.

'Nah, that's how you get into my life. Your name has to rhyme with those I love,' said Danny. 'So if you're staying put, you'll either have to change your name to Losie, to rhyme with Rosie, or Lat.'

'I quite like Losie,' said Lilah. 'What about the baby, though?'

'Oh, you think we should save Losie for the baby?' said Nat with a grin.

They laughed and Matt pulled his seat in closer, lifting his hand from Lilah's lap and draping it around the back of her chair. Lilah pressed her lips together to keep herself steady, subtly leaning into him.

An hour later, Lilah stepped out of the pub and into the pouring rain.

'Oh no!' She stepped back inside, straight into Matt who instinctively put an arm out, almost catching her in the process. He considered the weather, glanced back into the pub and tutted. Danny and Nat had left fifteen minutes earlier, so they couldn't get a lift home from them.

'It's not far,' he suggested. 'We could order an Uber?'

'Don't be ridiculous,' said Lilah, stepping out into the rain and pulling Matt with her. 'It's only a bit of wet.'

Matt went willingly, smiling as Lilah pulled him along, before catching up. Their smiles dropped as the rain started to soak through their clothes, and they walked hunched up. A cold wind blew against them and Matt made a noise, wrapping an arm around Lilah and drawing her close.

'Whose idea was this?' he shouted into the wind. 'Just a bit of wet?'

'And wind!' Lilah shouted back, hoping his arm always stayed around her, despite the fact that it was pressing her wet clothes into her skin.

'You know, I could have ordered an Uber to take you home and then me home,' came Matt's voice.

Lilah hesitated and then glanced at him.

'Oh.'

'Oh?'

'I just... I thought you might want to... not go

home tonight.'

Matt's stare was warm against her cheek as she looked forward, avoiding his gaze.

'Yeah?' was all he said.

She smiled and pushed on through the wind and rain. The sooner they got home, the sooner something could happen.

There were no more words until Lilah had opened the front door to the flat, they'd stepped inside, and she'd locked it behind them. Dripping on the front door mat and first step, they looked at each other, both soaked through, hair plastered to their faces, breathing hard.

Matt was the first to laugh, Lilah joining him.

'Might need a towel,' he murmured.

'Or a hot shower,' she agreed, taking off her shoes and peeling away her useless coat. Matt did the same, then followed as Lilah led them up the stairs. She turned up the heating as she passed the thermostat.

'What would you like first? A shower or a cup of tea?' It wasn't what she'd meant to offer, but the words had spilled out.

'A towel and a tea will do me,' he said, trying not to drip on the carpet. 'Then I'd best go home, I guess.'

'Don't be silly. You can stay here, if you want.' Lilah found two big towels and threw one to Matt before vanishing into the kitchen and staring at her kettle. How did one get someone they liked into bed with them? A cup of tea, stripping off wet clothes and a chat. Would that do it? She filled the kettle and turned it on.

'You know,' came Matt's voice, making her jump. She turned and found him in the doorway, towelling his hair, leaving it sticking up at odd angles. 'We never did talk about that kiss, did we.' He avoided her gaze, rubbing the towel over his clothes as if that would stop them dripping.

'We didn't,' said Lilah, her gaze running over his chest covered by his woollen jumper. She pulled a face. 'This isn't connected, not really, but we should get out of the wet clothes. Shouldn't we? We can't sit around drinking tea while damp.'

Matt gave something of a lopsided half smile that made Lilah swallow hard, and then he pulled his jumper over his head. Goosebumps immediately appeared on his arms, his t-shirt clinging to his chest. Lilah knew she shouldn't stare, but it was too late.

After a moment, she pulled off her own jumper and Matt's gaze was drawn down to her wet chest and the top of her dress.

'We should talk about that kiss,' he said, his voice deeper than before, and he took a small step inside the kitchen.

'We should,' Lilah agreed breathlessly, also stepping forward.

Her body was aching, a shiver running down her that probably had just as much to do with the cold as the proximity to Matt. She took another step and closed the gap between them just as the kettle clicked off. Neither of them looked at it, they only watched each other.

Lilah wanted Matt to move forward and take her in his arms, for them to kiss hurriedly, for him to lift her onto the kitchen worktop where she could welcome him in.

But he didn't move.

So, she moved forward, reaching up until he leaned down and their lips met, filling her senses with a strange wet heat that went all the way down to between her legs. Her body ached to be touched, but Matt kept his arms by his side, or wherever they were. They weren't on her.

Lilah wrapped her arms around his neck and pulled him deeper into the kiss, their tongues touching and Matt gave out an involuntary groan. Finally, his arms snaked around her waist, holding her close.

Lilah started plucking at his wet t-shirt and he allowed her to pull it over his head until he stood in her kitchen topless and damp.

They stared at one another, breathing hard.

'You want to do this?' he managed.

Lilah nodded.

'Definitely.'

She kissed him again, her hands on his cold chest, before she remembered herself and pulled away.

'Do you? We don't have to. You can stay in the spare bed again, if you prefer. I don't want to pressure you or—'

Matt's lips on hers shut her up and his hands searched her back for a way of ridding them of her dress.

'It's a zip,' she mumbled into the kiss.

'Got it,' he mumbled back, and they laughed as Matt unzipped her dress, dropping his kisses down to her neck as the dress had to be peeled from her. She reached for his jeans, but they were so soaked she couldn't undo them. He did it for her and then held out his hand.

'Bedroom?' he suggested.

She nodded, too busy staring at Matt in his underwear to make a noise.

They fell onto her bed, kissing and touching, the heat of their bodies making their skin sticky in the best way as they removed their underwear and Matt began exploring Lilah with groping hands and soft lips. She lay on her back, biting her lip, her hands in his gloriously floppy hair, watching his tongue on her nipple, when he stopped and glanced up at her.

'I don't have any protection,' he admitted.

Lilah looked around at the boxes that surrounded her bed and tried to remember what was where.

'I do,' she murmured. 'Somewhere.'

'Don't tell me you haven't unpacked them yet,' he said, glancing at the boxes.

'You haven't even bought them yet!' she told him

with a grin.

Matt laughed and shrugged.

'They're at my parents. Want me to go get them?' He gave her nipple a lick and Lilah shivered with pleasure.

'No, no, no. I've got some.'

She pulled herself away from him and padded barefoot around the bedroom, searching for a specific box. 'You didn't think to bring some, given that we were going to the pub and a quiz?'

'I wasn't expecting the rain and for you to invite me in and take off my clothes,' Matt told her with a grin. 'Honestly, not wanting to spoil the mood,' he continued as Lilah vanished into the hallway to search the boxes in the spare room, 'I thought I'd mention that kiss and you'd say you just wanted to be friends and that'd be that.'

Lilah smiled as she found the right box and dug around inside, finding the box of condoms among the other toiletries waiting to be unpacked.

'Why would I want to just be friends with the hot guy who owns the shop downstairs?' she told him, rushing back in and jumping on the bed. She crawled over to him and kissed his lips hard, passing him the condom packets she'd extracted.

'Really?'

'Really.' She lay back on the bed and gestured to her breasts. 'As you were.'

Matt laughed and almost pounced on her, putting his whole mouth over her breast.

Lilah watched him, grinning, until he moved back up her body and kissed her lips, his hand slipping between her legs. She moaned and pulled him closer, her hands over his arms, relishing the feel of him over her, between her legs, wrapping around him, not wanting this to end.

21

The wind was howling when Matt woke the next morning. It battered against the window, waking him, but Matt didn't mind. He found himself in Lilah's bed, her naked body pressed up against his, her eyes closed, mouth open, in what looked like a deep sleep. He studied her a moment, then carefully lifted the covers slightly to look down at their bodies next to one another. He spent too long staring at her breasts pressed between the bed sheet and her arm until, feeling a little like a voyeur, he lowered the covers and looked up at the ceiling. He took a deep breath, closed his eyes and went back to that night and the taste of Lilah, the sounds she made, the way it felt being inside her.

When he glanced back to her, he found her watching him with bleary eyes.

'Morning,' he whispered.

'Hello,' she murmured, closing her eyes and shuffling closer until her head rested on his chest. He wrapped his arms around her, relishing her hot, soft skin beneath his fingers, stroking her gently. Her hand moved down his chest, over his stomach to his groin and she gave a small noise of appreciation when she found that Matt was, in fact, very awake. He echoed her noise as she wrapped her hand around him and began to play, gently kissing his chest.

Matt leaned back and closed his eyes, smiling to himself.

By the time they'd dragged themselves out of bed, showered, fallen back into bed, dressed and Lilah had made them a coffee each, Matt's whole body was tingling. The smile wouldn't shift from his face, and he led the way down to his shop to open for what was left of the day.

They drank coffee over the counter, as they did most days, except this time Matt knew what Lilah looked like naked, and he couldn't get the thought out of his head.

'We never did talk about that kiss,' said Lilah, her hands wrapped around her coffee cup.

'Oh, I think we did.'

She smiled.

'I guess now we have to talk about the sex, instead?'

Matt filled his mouth with black coffee and glanced around the empty shop.

'What's there to talk about?' he said absentmindedly. He needed more customers. How was he ever going to move out of his parents' house if he didn't earn enough to find somewhere else to live? Renting was impossible, which meant building a deposit and buying.

'Well, are we just neighbours who have sex now?'

'No!' Matt returned his focus to Lilah and pushed his thoughts away. 'I mean, is that what you want?'

'Not really. Is it what you want?'

'No.' Matt fiddled with his cup. 'What do you want?'

'Honestly? I want to fall in love, get married, live happily ever after. Although I'm not sure if that's what happens,' Lilah added quietly.

'Happened for Danny and Nat.'

'True.' Lilah watched him for a moment, and he watched her back, admiring how her hair fell around her shoulders, a wisp always out of place near her ear. 'What do you want?'

'You,' he said without thinking. Mentally shaking himself, he cleared his throat. 'I want what you said, what Danny has. I always have. To fall in love, to find a wife and best friend, someone beautiful who makes me laugh who I can have loads of sex with, to make this business a roaring success and die old and happy, surrounded by my children, grandchildren and stunner of a wife.'

'Is that the same wife you started off with?'

'Oh yes, she only gets more beautiful with age. Like a good wine.'

Lilah gave Matt a look.

'What do you know about wine?'

He shrugged, giving her a grin.

'What do I know about women?'

'More than you think,' she mumbled into her coffee, giving him a sly smile.

His body reacted and he did his best to ignore it.

'I think you're the only woman who thinks that.'

'If only I could get more attractive the older I get,' said Lilah wistfully.

'Can't imagine you ageing any other way,' Matt told her matter-of-factly. 'You're already more beautiful today than you were when we met at the funeral. At... Lillian's funeral.' Matt's words drifted away and he looked back into the shop, almost missing the soft, hungry look Lilah gave him. 'Do you think Lillian's still here? Did she hear us last night?' he whispered.

Lilah joined him in looking around the shop.

'She's been quiet for a couple of days now,' she told him. 'I think that's my fault.'

'Why?'

'I've been sort of talking her ear off.' Lilah shrugged. 'I missed you.'

'Missed me? Where did I go?' Matt blinked and put his coffee cup down.

'To your parents.'

That first night at his parents came back in a rush to Matt and he stared at the counter as Lilah continued, 'I didn't know you were sleeping down here but then when you weren't, I felt, sort of, lonely. It's stupid. I'm sorry. But then I talked to Lillian a lot and she vanished too.' She sighed. 'I didn't mean to push her away.'

'You missed me sleeping down here?' Matt said gently.

Lilah's eyes widened.

'Oh, no, I don't want to push you away too.'

Matt laughed.

'You're not pushing me away. It's sweet.'

'It's weird.'

'I like weird.' Matt reached out and took Lilah's hand, bringing it to his lips and brushing a kiss over her skin. Just that small amount of contact was enough to make him want to pull her closer, or maybe lead her to the back room. His sleeping bag was gone, but who needed a sleeping bag for what he wanted to do?

'So, you want a relationship,' Lilah murmured hesitantly, her hand still in his. 'You want to give this a go?'

'Yes. Please. Do you?'

She nodded emphatically.

'Yes, please.'

They stared at each other in silence for a moment, and Matt was about to suggest his back room idea when his phone buzzed against the counter. It was a message from his mother, asking him if he'd be home that evening and if so, could he cook.

'Everything okay?' came Lilah's sweet voice.

He nodded.

'Yeah, sure.' He locked his phone, hiding the message behind a blank screen. 'Reckon we're too old to have sex on the floor?' The words spilled out before he'd had time to think, and he looked up into Lilah's eyes, shocked at himself.

She laughed.

'Speak for yourself,' she told him, stepping towards the back of the shop. 'Only one way to find out. But lock the door.'

Matt had never closed his shop so quickly. He found his note that said he'd be back in five minutes, considered changing the time, realised he was probably overestimating himself, then rushed to follow Lilah to the back of the shop.

Three minutes later they discovered that they were, in fact, too old to have sex on the threadbare carpet of the back room, but somehow still young enough to do it up against the wall. It was better, Lilah told him afterwards, it meant fewer carpet burns and it was easier on the knees.

Matt found he didn't have the words to reply, just a stupid grin that he couldn't shift, even as he reopened the shop and the first customers of the day came in.

'Hey,' he called to Lilah sitting in Stanley's armchair as the third customer left with a bag of stocking fillers. 'Fancy coming with me to Danny and Nat's Friends' Christmas Dinner? It's like Christmas Day but just with a small group of friends. But you might get asked a lot of, erm, questions. So, I understand if you don't want to.'

'What kind of questions?'

'Oh, you know, the usual. Are you sure you want to be with a grown man who owns a comic book shop? How many kids do you want? When are we getting married? That sort of stuff.'

Matt had kept his eyes down as he talked, filling in his stock spreadsheet with that day's sales and trying to not pay attention to the grand total figure of his income that month. It was down from last year. He'd have to do something about that.

It came as a shock to find Lilah on her feet and standing on the other side of the counter. She leaned across to him.

'I'd love to,' she told him. 'And yes, I want to be with a grown man who owns and runs a successful, interesting business.'

'Ha.' He glanced at that income number again. 'Successful, huh.'

'You're doing better than me right now. I have a date with Bea, so I best be going. Do you want to stay over tonight?' she asked him.

'In your spare bed?' Matt tested.

Lilah blew him a kiss and Matt closed the laptop with a thunk to watch her leave the shop, glancing back to him over her shoulder and giving him only seconds to wipe that silly smile off his face before more customers rang the bell over the door.

22

The next day and night were spent happily wrapping presents, placing them under the Christmas tree and spending time with Matt, both in and out of bed. Lilah was so happy that she caught herself humming on several occasions, so who knew how often she was humming without realising.

Matt pointed it out to her once, that she was humming a Christmas song while making cups of tea in the flat's kitchen. For a moment there, he'd thought it was Lillian.

Lillian had gone awfully quiet.

This was what Lilah was thinking about as she sipped her cup of tea, standing by the living room window and looking out across the town's rooftops towards the sea. Matt was just below, in his shop, and every now and then she would spot a customer heading inside or leaving. At one point, Stanley left with a bag of goodies, held close against the coastal winter wind. Matt claimed he'd told Stanley about the naked paintings in the gallery, apparently Stanley knew all about them, thank you very much.

Everything was running smoothly. Lilah's painting was coming along, although she was impatient to improve and start selling with Bea at local markets, to see if she could make an income. She'd need a job at some point. The bills couldn't be paid with good artistic intentions alone, but the thought of applying for jobs, going for interviews and getting rejected over and over filled her with the kind of dread that made her tea go cold.

She glanced back into the flat, over her shoulder, to the door of the second bedroom. What would it be like to have a flatmate? Someone else in her home, making noise, complaining about Matt being there. Unless the someone else was Matt...

Something touched her foot and her heart jumped. She looked down without spilling any tea – which she was quite proud about – and blinked at the yellow rose petal on the floor. It had fallen from the yellow roses still in their vase on the windowsill, the bunch that Matt had bought her soon after she'd moved in. That wasn't too long ago, was it? Yet, how long did roses usually last?

Lilah bent and picked up the petal, running her fingers over the velvet softness as it started to disintegrate.

'Lillian? Are you still here?' she said into the empty flat. 'Did you have unfinished business? Have you... finished it?' Lilah sighed and looked back down to the street, bringing her cup to her lips and freezing. The cup still touching her mouth, she watched in mild horror as her parents, Louise and Geoff Montgomery, walked against the wind down the pavement, past Matt's shop, and stopped outside the flat. Her father was bundled up in a coat and a hat threatening to fly off, and carrying a large suitcase that he seemed to regret. Her mother was leading the way, holding on to her own hat by pressing it to her head, and carrying only a hand-bag. She reached into the bag and pulled out a phone, pressing a button and holding it to her ear.

Lilah's phone rang.

She stared at her mother's name for a moment and then answered it, looking back out to her parents on the street.

'Hi.'

'Lilah! We're here!'

'What?' Lilah's voice lacked the surprise she was trying to fake, but then, she wasn't trying hard. Her mind was spinning too fast.

'We decided to come early. Surprise!'

'Early,' Lilah repeated breathlessly.

'Yes! Are you home? Can we come in?' Louise looked up and caught sight of her daughter in the window. She waved.

Lilah gave a feeble wave in return and then looked back into the flat. The untidy, very much not ready for her parents flat.

'I'm not—'

'I know, I know. I should have called. I just wanted to surprise you.'

A smile lifted the corners of Lilah's lips.

'Okay. It's okay. Of course, it's lovely you're early. I'll come down, hang on.'

Lilah hung up and rushed down the stairs to open the front door and get her parents in from the cold. She stepped outside to let them in the small porch and searched for Matt through the shop window. He caught her eye from behind the counter and she flashed him a smile, raised her hands in a shrug, then followed her parents inside and closed the front door.

She'd message him when she could.

'It's so nice being back here,' said her mother, stepping off the stairs and into the living room. She turned, looking around, until she faced Lilah. 'You've done nothing to it.'

'Not yet, no. I was taking my time going through Lillian's things. But the spare room is... not ready. I wasn't expecting you today.'

'Still, you could have vacuumed.'

Lilah gave her mother a look, and her mother raised her hands in surrender.

'Sorry. Sorry. I should have told you we were coming.'

'I told her to tell you,' Geoff told her gently, placing a kiss on his daughter's head. 'How're you doing?'

'Good. I'm good. Chuck your bags in your room

and I'll put the kettle on. It won't take me long to make the bed and give everything a clean.'

'Don't be silly. We can make the bed and help clean.'

'Tea first, though, surely?' said Geoff, looking to his wife almost aghast.

'Of course! And a sit down.' Louise plonked on the sofa and gazed around the living room at Lillian's art on the walls. 'Oh. Yellow roses.' Her eyes shone as she smiled up at Lilah. 'Lil's favourites. That's thoughtful of you.'

'Actually, Matt gave them to me.'

'Matt? What? The man downstairs?'

For a moment Lilah thought her mother might jump up and rush down the stairs to the shop and Lilah would have to run after her, but neither moved. They remained still, in silence, Geoff looking from one to the other.

'He gave you yellow roses?' Louise continued.

'Yeah, to apologise.' Lilah snapped her mouth shut, then tried again. 'To welcome me to the town.'

Her mother narrowed her eyes.

'Apologise for what?'

'Welcoming me to the town,' Lilah repeated, stepping back and vanishing into the kitchen. She rested her hands on the worktop and dropped her head between her arms, allowing herself a small groan.

'Everything okay?' Her father walked in and placed a comforting hand on her shoulder as he reached for the mugs and set out three.

'Yup.' Lilah stood up straight and popped tea bags into the cups.

'Sorry we came early. I did try to tell her...'

'It's okay. Really. I mean, nothing's clean yet. But it's okay.'

'We don't mind about that.' He gave her a smile. 'I'll do this. Go chat with your mum. She misses you.' Lilah stepped out of her father's way but stayed in the kitchen. 'I miss you too,' he added.

'I know.' She gave him a quick hug from behind. 'I miss you both. I'm glad you're here.'

She ventured back into the living room where her mother was looking at one of Lillian's framed photos of them together in their twenties, arms interlocked.

'Are you okay?' Lilah asked gently. 'Should I have tidied everything away?'

'No.' Louise had tears in her eyes, but they didn't fall. 'It's like she's still here.'

It was on the tip of Lilah's tongue to tell her mother about the possibility of Lillian's ghost, she was about to say that Lillian was still there, but then there was the doubt. Was Lillian still there?

'Did Matt know Lillian's favourite colour is yellow?'

Lilah nodded, sitting on the sofa.

'Of course. They were quite close. It's why she left him the shop.' She didn't mention that Lillian had also promised him the flat. No one else needed to know that.

'What did he have to apologise for?'

'Oh, nothing. We were short with each other when we met, that's all,' Lilah managed. 'He's grieving too. Did you know Lillian had art up in the local gallery?'

'What? No!'

'Yeah. They're nudes.'

'Nudes! Anyone we know? Not this Matt fellow?'

Lilah laughed a little too loud, just as her father brought in the cups of tea on a tray and placed it on the coffee table. Her mother helped herself as Geoff dropped into an armchair.

'No. Stanley.' Lilah smiled as her mother's cup stopped halfway to her lips. 'That's what I was thinking.' Lilah leaned forward, putting her cup back on the table. 'Lillian mentioned a Stan, didn't she.'

'Nudes, you say,' Louise mused and sipped her tea. 'What's this Matt like, then? He bought her flowers,' she added to Lilah's father. He only raised his eyebrows and drank his tea.

'He's nice. You'll like him. What did Lillian tell you about Stanley?'

'Oh, I'm sure we will. Lillian obviously liked him enough to leave him her shop. Says a lot about him. And it's a comic book shop, is it?'

'Yeah, among other things. What did Lillian tell you about Stanley, Mum?'

'What kind of other things?'

'You can look when you next go down. Mum, what did Lillian tell you about Stanley?'

Her mother sighed and put down her cup.

'She mentioned him a few times. Said he was a nice older gentleman she'd come to befriend. That's all.'

That wasn't all. It was obvious that wasn't all.

'And?' Lilah probed.

'And nothing else.'

Mother and daughter stared at one another, as Geoff stared blankly between them.

'When are we going to meet this Matt?' Louise broke the silence.

'Whenever you want.' Lilah snapped back to reality. 'I'll just let him know you're here.' She had to give him a heads up that he couldn't stay that night, and she didn't want any awkwardness. At least, not as much awkwardness as Matt staying the night would cause. She found her phone and typed out a message, explaining her parents had come early without warning and that they'd love to meet him. Lilah hit send before she realised she hadn't told her parents about their budding relationship, and Matt didn't know that.

'Erm,' she accidentally said out loud.

'Erm?'

Should she tell Matt not to mention anything about them being together? What if he didn't see them as together? No, they'd had a whole discussion about it. But it was too early, wasn't it?

What if Matt was offended that she didn't want to tell her parents yet?

'Erm.'

'What's wrong?' her mother asked.

'I just need to, erm, go make your bed. You stay here. Relax. I'll go make your bed and then maybe you could go check out the gallery while I clean? It might be closed but the coffee shop next door is lovely.' Lilah stood and fretted for a moment. 'Matt and I are seeing each other,' she said quickly before dashing out of the room and into the spare bedroom.

'What?' Louise called after her, but Lilah didn't go back to repeat herself. She'd follow Lilah in if she wanted to talk about it, which is exactly what happened.

'You're seeing the man in the shop?' her mother murmured, sliding into the bedroom and closing the door behind her. As if Lilah's father couldn't possibly find out that his daughter, in her thirties, could be dating and sleeping with someone.

'Yes.'

'What does that mean? You're dating?'

Lilah pulled a face. That wasn't her favourite word, but she didn't know how else to explain what they were doing at this stage. Spending time together and having sex didn't feel like the right label to give her mother.

'Er, yeah.'

Louise gasped.

'You're having sex with him!' she whispered fiercely, leaning across the bed to get closer to Lilah, who was pulling clean bedding out of the wardrobe.

'Mum!

'Well, you are, aren't you?'

'Yeah, but you don't need to say it out loud.'

Louise straightened and beamed.

'Lillian would be so proud.'

Lilah laughed despite herself and they both looked up as the lightbulb over the bed flickered twice.

23

Although his legs wanted nothing more than to close the shop and run, Matt managed to convince them to stay put, behind the counter, as he waited for Lilah to emerge from the flat with her parents. It wasn't what he was used to in a relationship: to meet the parents a couple of days after seeing their daughter naked for the first time. That was definitely a thought he had to push from his mind.

'Lillian, if you're still here, I could really use your help,' he said under his breath, glancing up quickly to check if anything moved or flickered in the shop.

Nothing did.

Matt blew out his cheeks and went back to staring at the spreadsheet on his laptop. In the middle of the shop, the large table was clear and set up, ready for that evening's DnD session. In the meantime, his December sales were still down and he needed to figure out a solution. What was the latest craze? What trend did he need to jump on? This was when a healthy social media habit came in handy, but Matt had never figured that conundrum out. As far as he knew, there was no such thing as a healthy social media habit and the whole social media thing made him nauseous. He had a couple of accounts for the shop, just to mention the latest DnD campaigns, gaming evenings and any new stock arrivals, but it wasn't enough. The whole thing tended to be pointless and he didn't have the energy or knowledge to improve it in any way.

No, he'd have to go old school and ask the young people who regularly ventured into the shop what they wanted to see. That was better, anyway, wasn't it? Proper customer research.

It still wouldn't be enough. He needed more people in the shop to buy things rather than more things to buy. How would he get more people inside, both in and out of season? Events were likely the answer. At least, they were the only answer he could come up with as his stomach turned with anxiety. He glanced up at the windows, but there was no one there. Lilah's front door was still shut.

Another DnD campaign? Maybe more board game nights. Or a weekend. Oh, a tournament! Matt wrote these ideas down on a notebook he kept on the counter for doodling.

When he next glanced up, a spark of yellow caught his attention. A petal lay on the floor near the door. That hadn't been there before, he was sure of it. He moved around the counter to pick it up.

'I'm guessing you're still here, Lil?' he asked the

empty shop. 'Be great to have your opinion on these ideas. I know I can ask Lilah, but she's busy... Well, you know, I bet you're upstairs too, huh?' Matt sighed. 'I miss you, Lil. I miss our chats.'

His chest tightened as he ran the petal through his fingers. It didn't go in the bin, instead he placed it next to the scribbled ideas on his notepad, as if that was how Lillian would see them.

'Stay with me through this,' he added, his voice strained, as movement caught his eye outside and the flat's front door opened. Lilah and her parents appeared, and Lilah gestured towards the shop door, catching Matt's eye for a moment before she turned away to lock the front door.

The door tinkled as her mother pushed open the door and immediately met Matt's eyes. He couldn't look away. She had Lilah's eyes, or rather, Lilah had her eyes, and it hit him then that neither of them had Lillian's eyes. That was probably a good thing. It would be strange to stare wistfully into the eyes of the woman who been such a role model and mother figure to him. He'd much rather stare into Lilah's eyes, so he wrenched himself away from her mother and glanced at her father, following close behind. Thankfully, Lilah then appeared and stepped ahead to introduce them.

'Mum, Dad, this is Matt. Matt, these are my parents, who arrived early.'

'Hi,' said Matt before anyone else could respond.

'So nice to meet you, Matt. I'm Louise, this is

Geoff. It's so lovely to meet the man my sister was obviously so fond of. And my daughter, apparently.' Lilah's mother held out a hand and Matt shook it, frozen other than his arm moving up and down once.

'Nice to meet you,' said Lilah's father, also shaking Matt's hand as he looked around the shop. 'Nice place you have here.'

'It's Lillian's shop! You've been here before,' said his wife.

'I know, but I like what he's done with it.' Lilah's father moved away to check out the shelves and Lilah watched, but stayed close to her mother and Matt. Which Matt was eternally grateful for.

'Sorry we came early,' said Louise. 'Feels like I won't be living that down, but I wanted to surprise Lilah.'

'You did!' said Lilah. 'And I don't mind. It's lovely you're here now.' She glanced at Matt and a tingle went through him as their eyes met.

'We don't want to get in the way. It's just that I miss Lillian, and my daughter, of course. It's nice to be back in Lillian's flat and shop.' Louise looked around. 'How are you finding it? Lillian often struggled, even at Christmas. If it wasn't summer, sales were down. That's what she always said.'

Matt relaxed a little and gave a small laugh.

'Yeah, I know that feeling. I was just trying to think of some events I could hold here, get more people inside.'

Both Lilah and her mother brightened, which sent off an alarm bell in Matt's head.

'I think a local comic con would be good. You could have a stall at others, too, around the country,' Lilah murmured, looking back for her father.

'Hmm.' Matt pulled a face. 'I tried that in the beginning. It's exhausting, especially by yourself, but I might have to go back to it.'

'I can help,' said Lilah with a sweet smile.

'What about Christmas-themed events?' Lilah's mother suggested. 'A Christmas party.'

'A Christmas... party,' Matt echoed slowly, hating every word.

'Yes!'

'As in, sell tickets to a party in the shop? Mum, I don't think—'

'No, no. You wouldn't sell tickets. But you could have a raffle. That would raise some money. Or you could do it for charity and raise the profile of the shop a bit. Some PR. Why not?'

Matt stared wide eyed as panic mixed with business sense, leaving him speechless.

'Erm...'

'You could start with a practise party, I guess,' Louise continued, looking at the nearby shelves. 'Invite friends and family. See how much of everything you'd need.'

'A bit like the quiz for Danny's football team,' Lilah added. 'Oh! Do a quiz in the shop!'

Matt smiled at her, lost for a moment in her eyes lighting up.

'Do you live locally?' Louise asked, pulling him back.

'Yes, on the other side of town.'

'That must be a pain.'

'It is.'

'Easy enough to drive, though. Maybe Matt could rent your spare room once we're gone? Give you an income while you're working on building an art business and give Matt a nice commute to work?' Lilah's mother looked at her and then seemed to realise what she'd said. 'Oh. But that would mean you two moving in together and you're probably not ready for that. Forget I said anything!' She raised her hands.

Matt wasn't really listening. He was thinking about how it was an easy enough drive, if you had a car, which he didn't. There also wasn't much parking around. When he came back to the conversation and looked up, Lilah was watching him, but he couldn't interpret her expression.

'So, we're going to the gallery to see the naked man Lillian painted, what else is there to do around here so close to Christmas?' Lilah's mother was asking.

'You've missed the last Christmas market,' said Lilah. 'And the quiz. I think that's it. Other than the pantomime.'

She met Matt's eyes again and he struggled to

focus on what they were talking about. He should be saying helpful things, but his mind had gone blank.

'Maybe I can help you go through Lillian's stuff? We could use some of her art in your new business.' Louise clapped her hands. 'Oh, and I can help you organise a party, if you like? I used to work in PR.'

Matt's eyes widened again and his mouth opened, but he wasn't quick enough with the words.

'He doesn't need PR for a practise party,' said Lilah.

'No, but the real thing will have to be quick if we're to do it before Christmas.'

'Maybe it's a New Year thing? Or a dark January event?

Lilah and her mother started chatting to one another, planning his event that he hadn't even said yes to, and all Matt could do was watch and wonder if he should be interjecting.

'Best to let them get on with it,' murmured Lilah's father, having worked his way around the shop and ended up at the counter. 'And I'll have this.' He placed a book on the counter and pulled out a wallet.

'Oh. Sure. Thanks.' It occurred to Matt to give him the book for free, but by the time he'd managed to figure out the words for such a thing, Lilah's father had paid, picked up the book, given the shop another accepting nod and found Stanley's armchair to wait for his wife to be ready.

Lilah and her mother were talking about drinks and food, how to keep costs down while giving everyone a good time.

'Erm...' ventured Matt.

Lilah caught herself.

'Mum, this really should be Matt's thing. Maybe we let him think about it?'

'Oh, of course! So lovely to meet you, Matt. Maybe we should all have dinner one night before the big day? Come on then, let's go to this gallery before it closes.'

Lilah's parents left the shop as Matt called after them, 'Lovely to meet you too!'

He turned to Lilah who was grinning. She wandered over, kissed his cheek and went to follow her parents.

'See you later,' she told him. 'I'll message you. We'll figure something out.'

Once again, Matt was alone in his shop, and it seemed quieter than before.

'Well. That was something,' he said into the silence.

As if in answer, from the back of the shop came the bang of something falling over when he knew that if he went to check, everything would be in its place.

'Exactly, Lil,' he responded, looking down at the yellow petal next to his notepad of event ideas. With a small laugh, he found his pen and added to the list, *Christmas quiz, Christmas party*.

24

It didn't take long for Lilah's mother to organise the little drinks evening at Matt's shop, once Lilah had talked privately with him about it to see if he really wanted to do it. They'd spent the previous night apart, and they'd spend this night apart. Which was the excuse Lilah was giving herself for clinging to Matt that evening as people started arriving at the shop. They'd added some more fairy lights to the shelves and filled the counter with bottles and red and green paper party cups, along with three trays of sliders and mince pies. Her father and Matt had gone through some of his stock and found enough to create a small raffle prize, and Lilah's mother was on the door with some homemade raffle tickets, selling them as people arrived.

Matt stood in the corner, staring at nothing. After Lilah had followed his line of sight, double checking he really was staring at nothing, she went over to join him.

'Everything okay?'

'Hmm? Hmm.'

'What's wrong?'

'Nothing.' Matt kept staring forward, not blinking.

'Is this happening too fast? You don't want to be doing this.'

'I just...'

Lilah waited, but Matt closed his mouth and sighed.

'Please tell me,' she murmured, shifting closer to him.

'I just didn't think everyone would be invited,' he whispered, his eyes suddenly darting to her mother on the door as Stanley walked in and a raffle ticket was thrust into his hand.

'But this is for friends and family.'

'Yeah.'

'Who didn't you want here? Stanley?' Lilah whispered back, watching as her mother brought Stanley round and he paid for the raffle ticket. She must have mentioned Lillian, because soon Stanley was nodding, and then said something that made her mother give a laugh that was tinged with grief.

'No. No, I like that Stanley's here.'

'Danny?'

Danny, Nat and Rosie were in the opposite corner, fussing over some books Rosie might be interested in.

'No, no. I'm glad they're here.'

'Then who?'

Danny straightened at that moment, glanced towards the door and left his wife and daughter to join Lilah and Matt.

'You invited your parents?'

Matt stiffened. Lilah looked between them.

'My mum must have,' she said, glancing up at Danny. 'Is it a problem? It gives them a chance to see how well Matt is doing.'

Danny only gave Matt a look and Matt did his best not to respond. He gave another sigh and stepped away, closer to the back room.

Panicked, Lilah looked to the shop door as an older man and woman entered. The man didn't seem fazed. He glanced around the shop, spotted the food and drinks on the counter and headed straight for them without talking to Lilah's mother. The woman, on the other hand, sneered and gingerly took the raffle tickets Louise offered. Lilah's mother's expression changed into something wooden and Lilah reached out, brushing her hand against Matt's. He took it and gave a little squeeze before dropping it and moving ever so slightly away.

'Is it really that bad?' she whispered. 'You're living with them.'

'There's a reason he didn't want to move back in with them,' said Danny, giving Lilah a shrug and heading back to his family. 'This'll be fun.'

Lilah heaved a sigh and turned on Matt.

'What do you want me to do? Can I get rid of

them?'

'No. No, it's okay. They're here now. For the first time. Ever.'

'What?' Lilah squeaked, her eyes wide. 'They've never been here before? You've had this shop for five years!'

Matt only nodded, then he took another step away and disappeared into the back room, closing the door behind him. Lilah watched him go, her heart pounding, and then looked to Danny. He gave her another shrug, but nothing more.

'Men,' she muttered, making her way over to her mother by the door. 'Slight problem,' she murmured as Matt's mother joined his father by the drinks, muttering in his ear.

'Matt's parents?' her mother asked.

'Apparently they've never even been here before.'

'Damn it. I should have asked him. That's my fault. Where is he?'

'In the back room.'

'Should I ask them to leave?'

'How can we?' Lilah glanced back to the counter. Her father was attempting to start a conversation and then, in a moment that made Lilah's insides freeze, both of Matt's parents turned and looked at her. 'I think Dad just told them I'm seeing their son.'

'Oh.'

'And I guess if they haven't seen the shop, maybe

he hasn't told them about us yet.'

'Ah.'

'Hmm. I might just, erm, go see if Matt's okay.'

'Really? You're going to leave us in this situation?' her mother hissed.

'You're doing great.' Lilah patted her arm. 'I'll try and be quick.'

She stepped lightly across the shop, watched by Matt's mother and Danny, and slid into the back room, closing the door behind her. Matt was standing by the kettle, staring blankly at it.

'I'm so, so sorry. And my mum is so, so sorry. She should have asked you. I should have asked you. I'm sorry. Are you okay?' Lilah stepped over to him and brushed a hand down his arm, wishing they were further along in their relationship so she could comfortably throw her arms around him. If they were further along, she might have known that inviting his parents was the wrong thing to do.

'You guys really don't get on, huh?' she tried uncertainly.

'Oh, we get on,' said Matt in a quiet voice. 'But they disagree with all of my life choices.' He blinked and looked up at her. 'Except you. They don't know about you. But I think they'll be happy about you.'

'Oh? Why's that?' Lilah fidgeted.

'That's what success is, isn't it. Meeting someone, getting married, giving them grandkids.'

Lilah stared at the carpet as Matt talked, the weight on her shoulders getting heavier with every word, although her mind was stuck on only one of the words.

'That's what you think success is?' she asked without looking up.

'I don't know. That's what they think it is. Plus a big job. Something that pays well. Something that isn't this, but I can't give them that. I can give them the rest of it. And now there's you.'

Lilah still didn't look up. The carpet was bordering on disgusting. It was threadbare and had obviously had so much dirt walked into it over the years that no vacuum could save it. Had Lillian had it put down, or did it predate her?

'Now there's me.' Lilah frowned. 'You are successful, you know.' She looked up and met Matt's eyes. 'This shop is amazing, and it's not your fault that your parents can't see that. Is that why you're with me? To tick that box and make your parents happy?'

'What? No! Of course it isn't. I'm with you because you're hot and you let me kiss you.'

There was a short pause and then Lilah laughed. Matt grinned playfully and took Lilah's hand. 'None of that has anything to do with you. Or us. Not really. It's just... my parents never really approve. But they'll approve of you.'

'I hope so,' said Lilah, closing the gap between them and looking up into Matt's soft eyes. 'Because I think my dad just told them about us.' She gave an apologetic smile.

Matt searched her eyes and she watched as a flicker of fear passed over him. Then he gave a shrug, leaned down and kissed her lips. It sent a shockwave of pleasure through her, so she stayed put, face tilted up in case he wanted to kiss her again.

'Good. Means I don't have to.' He gave her another quick kiss.

'Will they be angry about that?'

'It's been less than a week. I didn't have a reason to tell them yet.' Their lips met again.

'True. Good. I'm sorry we invited them.'

'How did you get their number?'

'I don't know. Mum must have asked Danny, I guess.'

'Then my quarrel is with him,' Matt declared before kissing her again, deeper this time. She wrapped her arms around his neck and pulled him close.

'We could stay here,' he said around the kiss.

'Hmm?'

'Have another go at making love on the floor.'

Lilah laughed, stepping away from him.

'This floor is disgusting. I have no idea how you slept on it for so long. And I'm not having sex in here while everyone we know is out there. Come on.'

She opened the door onto the shop just a little and peered through. 'Bea's here!' She grinned, her heart leaping. 'I need to introduce my mum to her properly. Let's go.'

'Okay. Right behind you.'

'You got this,' she told Matt, squeezing his hand. He squeezed back, took a deep breath and they stepped into the shop.

'Lilah! I've just met Bea!'

Lilah went straight to her mother and Bea and began excitedly introducing them, telling her mother everything she could about her painting sessions with Bea and the markets she and Lillian used to attend, even though her mother already knew everything.

'And I see you've met Stanley,' said Bea.

'Oh, yes, what a lovely man. A good friend of Matt's,' said Lilah's mother.

'And of Lillian.'

Lilah's mother's eyes widened.

'Of course, he's the naked man,' she whispered.

Bea and Lilah laughed.

'I showed them the paintings in the gallery. Apparently, Stanley knew all about them,' Lilah explained.

'That doesn't surprise me,' said Bea. She went to say more when a raised voice from across the shop stopped her. The party fell silent except for Matt's mother.

'I don't see why you don't sell!'

'Because this is my shop, Mum. This is my dream.'

'Some dream. A tacky little place filled with toys.'

'Oi!' shouted Lilah's mother. 'This place isn't tacky. This was my sister's shop before she gave it to your son.'

'And what did she sell? Did she sell toys, too? They're not even good children's toys. You cater to grown men, Matthew. It's horrible.' Matt's mother gestured at Stanley as she spoke and Lilah held her breath as Stanley raised an eyebrow.

'And we have to hear about your new relationship from your girlfriend's father. Are we not good enough to tell? Or are you just keeping her sweet so you can move in upstairs and move out of your old bedroom?'

There was a collective gasp and the group, as one, glanced at Lilah. Heat burned her chest, rising up her neck to her cheeks. Matt met her eyes for one terrible moment and then he returned his attention to his mother, his fists curled at his sides.

Louise went to speak at the same time as Matt, but Stanley's loud, calm voice drowned them out.

'How very dare you, madam. Your son has created the most welcoming community hub this town has, for people who think differently and dare to dream. He's a god send, is what he is. Lillian saw it the moment she met him. What a shame that you, as his own mother, can't see it. You should be ashamed of yourself. Not once have you ever set foot in this shop, despite all the invitations, and when you finally do it's to raise your voice at your son's promise and success, and to speak down about Lillian and her wonderful niece. You don't hear me complaining about not knowing he and Lilah had started courting, despite the fact that Matt mentioned Lilah to me on a number of occasions when she moved in.'

Lilah glanced at Matt and he looked away hurriedly.

'I, for one, am incredibly happy for them and wish them only the best. As I know Lillian would have done. Perhaps if you cannot be happy for your son's success in this shop, you should not have come. And stop being such a Grinch!'

Everyone slowly turned to Matt's mother who looked like she might explode.

'Well...' she started, trembling.

Lilah inhaled sharply, wishing she could defend her somehow, despite the things she'd said.

'I think we should go,' said Matt's father, putting down his drink and taking his wife's hand. 'I will not have my wife talked to like that.' He gave Matt a pointed look and began to lead Matt's mother out.

Lilah's parents stood aside.

'Oh, please, don't...' Lilah tried, moving to follow them.

'Wait,' said Matt calmly, following his parents and ushering them outside. It was cold out there, and dark, and Lilah went to follow when her mother held her back.

'It needed to be said,' she told Lilah.

'I know. Thank you, Stanley.' She turned back

into the shop. 'I appreciate it. But I need to make sure Matt's okay.'

They let her go and she tentatively pushed open the shop door to hear Matt talking to his parents. He was apologising but also pointing out the truth in what Stanley had said.

'Well, I'm sorry you feel that way,' said his mother, looking past him to Lilah. 'We didn't even get to meet you.'

'And yet you shouted that I'm using her,' Matt said.

His mother blinked and recoiled a little.

'Yes. I'm sorry about that.' She met Lilah's eyes. 'I'm sorry.'

'I'm sorry, too,' said Matt. 'About all that. Do you want to come back in? Start again?'

'No. I don't think so. Enjoy your little party.' His mother met Lilah's eyes again and Lilah attempted a smile.

'It was nice to meet you,' she said lamely. 'I'm sorry about all that.'

'Hmm.'

Matt's parents left without more words or hugs and, unable to stop herself, Lilah slipped her arms around Matt's waist.

'I'm so sorry. Do you want to go after them?'

'No, it's okay. That's just how they are.'

'They didn't hug you.'

'They haven't hugged me since I was little.'

Lilah's chest hurt and she held Matt tighter,

pushing her face into his arm.

'Sorry,' she mumbled into his jumper.

He smiled and turned so he could hug her back, and there they stayed, holding each other tightly, until the cold night air got beneath their clothes and Lilah's mother made them go back into the warmth of the shop.

25

'Maybe we shouldn't go,' said Matt as Lilah walked over to the shop counter. It was the day after the party, and closing time. Lilah had come downstairs so they could leave for Danny's Friends' Christmas Dinner, and her expression fell as he spoke. He focused on hiding his laptop away in his safe and turning off the fairy lights.

'Is this about last night?' she asked, watching him until he was forced to look up and meet her eyes.

He sighed.

'I don't know. Maybe. No.'

'Maybe, no?'

'I'm just not in a Christmas party mood.' He looked around the shop, searching for something else to do, but everything was tidy, put away and turned off. No one would have known there had been a party there the night before, and Matt wished he could say the same about him. That night, lying in bed in his childhood room that now resembled a bed and breakfast, he replayed the night's events over and over, wishing he'd grabbed his sleeping bag and stayed in the shop's back room. He'd tried talking to his parents when he'd gotten home, but his mother had already gone to bed and his father just brushed his words away. He didn't want Matt's apologies or reasons.

That morning, Matt had woken early, unsure if he'd even slept, and had another go at talking to his mother. She'd been more open, letting him apologise, but telling him how hurt she'd been.

Matt had pointed out that her raised words had hurt him, his girlfriend and customers, to which his mother repeated how hurt she was that he hadn't told her about Lilah.

They'd left on good terms, without the hug, which was to be expected. After that, all Matt could think about was the hug Lilah had given him the night before, after his parents walked away.

'I understand that,' Lilah was saying in a gentle tone.

Matt hesitated. There was an argument brewing inside him, and he was unsure of whether he wanted Lilah close at that moment – another hug wouldn't go amiss – or if he wanted to be alone. He certainly didn't want to go home to his parents that night, and he couldn't stay with Lilah with her parents in the flat. He'd fetched his sleeping bag into work that day, fearing this outcome.

'Maybe being among friends will help? Danny

knows how to cheer you up.'

Matt flinched inwardly.

'I don't think I need cheering up.'

Lilah gave him a look that made him decide on the being alone option, and he bristled, resisting the urge to stomp into the back room and close the door until she left.

'It's just complicated,' he told her. 'And we can't just magically fix over three decades of this suddenly before Christmas. And I can't rely on Danny to cheer me up. What if I don't want to be cheered up? Last night was a lot.' The words were spilling out now and the alarm bells in Matt's head were sounding, getting louder as he continued. 'I don't even know why we threw that party. It didn't do anything for the business. It just cost me more money and got me into this mess. My parents were humiliated—'

'But your mum started shouting at you! And saying horrible things. We couldn't just sit by and watch that happen.'

'But it's been happening one way or another my whole life,' Matt proclaimed, his voice rising. 'You just sit and take it and stay quiet and eventually it goes away.'

'But it doesn't, does it? It doesn't go away because it's been going on your whole life!'

They stared at each other, hot tears pricking the back of Matt's eyes. He was determined they wouldn't fall, especially in front of Lilah.

'Look, I get where you're coming from, and it's nice that you want to help—'

'Of course I do, you're amazing and you deserve better.'

Matt stopped and searched her eyes.

'You really think that?'

Lilah softened and smiled, reaching out to him. He let her take his hand and she brushed a soft thumb over his skin, sending a wave of comfort and pleasure through him.

'Can we just get Christmas over with?' he murmured, blinking hard.

'Okay. But come out tonight. You'll have fun.'

There was some truth in this, Matt knew. It would be fun tonight, if he could just stop feeling this way, and Danny was probably his best bet at being distracted from it all. A small group of people gathered in one place, with his best friend, and finally Matt wouldn't be the only one there still single. He squeezed Lilah's hand and gave a small nod.

'Okay. Fine. But maybe we just stay for food?'

'Of course. We don't have to stay long.' Lilah squeezed his hand back. 'Ready?'

Matt had been right from the beginning. Coming out had been a mistake. A couple of hours after leaving the shop, they stood in Danny's house surrounded by three other couples, mostly people

Danny and Nat knew from their respective jobs, discussing parenting and holidays. He'd thought it would be different doing this with a girlfriend, but nothing had changed other than every now and then the girlfriend would look over and give him a smile.

There were only so many times he could smile and nod about someone he didn't know well telling him how wonderful their child was.

Finally, he escaped, after what felt like hours but turned out to be only ten minutes. Not that he was clock watching. Matt made his way to the table with the drinks, next to a beautifully decorated Christmas tree that put his to shame, and grabbed a beer from the cooler on the floor. The house smelled delicious, of nutmeg and cinnamon and the cooking of roast turkey and potatoes. As he opened the beer, wishing he'd suggested a leaving signal to Lilah, he turned and came face-to-face with Danny.

'Hey!'

'Hi,' Matt managed, filling his mouth with beer before he could shout an eagle cry to Lilah, on the other side of the room, talking to a woman she didn't know and managing to look animated and interested. How did she do that?

'I'm really glad you came. Dinner's ready soon. How are you? After last night and everything.'

'All right.'

Danny gave his friend a hard look.

'Matty. It's me. I know you're not all right.'

'I'm fine. My parents aren't talking to me much and I'm down the cost of food and drinks and nothing good actually came from it all, but I'm fine.'

A silence filled the gap between them.

'Sorry,' said Danny eventually. 'Do you need help to cover the costs?'

'No. No, that's not really the problem.' Matt sighed. 'Guess I'm just annoyed I ever agreed to the thing.' His gaze landed on Lilah again, across the room. 'It was Lilah's mother's suggestion. She organised the whole thing. She invited them.'

'It wasn't her fault. She didn't know.'

'No. Guess I should just wear a t-shirt that says "Don't invite my parents!"' Matt grumbled, moving away from Danny.

Danny didn't follow, but Matt caught him shaking his head. The ball of rage in his gut took on a new life, so he left his drink on a shelf and rushed to the toilet, locking himself in. It was the downstairs toilet, so it was small. Just a cupboard with a toilet, sink and a mirror. He stared at his own miserable reflection, trying to ignore the anger in his own eyes, then splashed cold water on his face and let it drip down his nose, back into the sink.

There came a gentle knock on the door.

'I'm in here,' Matt called gently, not trusting himself to talk louder.

'I know. It's me,' came Lilah's voice. 'Are you okay?'

Matt clenched his eyes shut. Couldn't he get a

moment alone?

'I'm fine.'

'Okay.'

There was a silence from outside and Matt took another breath, glancing up to meet his own eyes in the mirror's reflection.

'What're you going to do?' he mumbled to it.

'Danny just told me off for letting my mum organise your party, that's all,' came Lilah's voice.

She hadn't left. She hadn't walked away. In the mirror, Matt's expression hardened and he stared at himself, not blinking.

'Okay,' he managed, gritting his teeth.

'I just don't think that's fair. Can we talk?'

'Bit busy at the moment.'

'Right.'

Another moment of silence stretched out between them as Matt searched his own eyes, wondering what he'd do next. Through the door, he heard Lilah sigh and with a soft growl, buried deep in his throat, he unlocked the door, opened it enough to find her, grabbed her arm and pulled her through.

'What the— What're you doing?' Lilah hissed as she fell against the wall and Matt closed the door as best he could.

'You wanted to talk.'

'Not in here! We don't fit.'

They would fit, Matt thought, if they weren't snarling at each other. It probably didn't bode well for the relationship if only days in they were having a hushed argument in his friend's downstairs toilet.

'You wanna go out there where everyone can hear?'

'Better than forming a queue!' Lilah opened the door. 'Come out when you've got your head screwed on.'

Matt almost screamed, staring at the door as she closed it behind her, breathing hard.

26

Unsure of whether Matt would follow, Lilah made her way to Danny, standing in the living room chatting to a couple of men.

'Danny?' she ventured.

He did a double take at her expression and then excused himself, guiding Lilah away. 'I think I'm going to go,' she told him quietly.

'Oh, why? Because of Matty?'

'He's really unhappy and it's my fault. I think it would be better if I leave.'

'But we're about to eat. You're hungry, right?'

'Yeah, and it smells amazing, but I don't want to make a scene.' As if in argument, Lilah's stomach chose that moment to rumble.

'You're not.'

'Matt's hiding in the toilet,' said Lilah bluntly.

Danny sighed.

'He's not normally like this,' he told her.

She gave him a strange look and smiled.

'You don't have to explain him. It's okay. Look, I

really like Matt. A lot. This is all my fault—'

'It isn't.'

'It is. I should have stopped my mum doing anything that involved his business. I don't know why I didn't. I just feel like Matt needs to not be near me right now and I hope he'll listen when he's ready and forgive me. But until then, I'm going to go. Thank you so much,' she added quickly, before Danny could argue, 'for inviting me. I really appreciate it. And this has been lovely. I don't want to put a dampener on anything, so I'll go quietly and see you again soon?'

Danny's gaze had drifted past Lilah, but if she stopped talking, she didn't know if she'd be able to remember everything she wanted to say and be able to say it without a tremble going into her voice.

'Hey,' said Matt.

She turned to him slowly and offered a smile, the best she could muster.

'You're leaving?' he asked.

'I think it's for the best.'

Matt's jaw was tense, so she looked back to Danny and gave him an apologetic smile. 'I'll go. Thanks again.'

'Sure, have a nice Christmas,' said Danny quietly.

'You too. See you next year!' Lilah moved to the front door where her coat was in a pile on the stairs, she fished around looking for it.

'I'll go with you.' Matt followed her.

'You don't have to go,' said Danny.

'I think it's for the best,' Matt echoed Lilah and she froze, her eyes prickling as they considered forming tears. She sighed, grabbed her coat and stepped out of the front door before she said something she regretted. Matt let her go, pulling on his own coat slowly.

'We haven't eaten yet,' Danny said quietly after her.

'Say bye to Nat for me. I'll talk to you tomorrow,' said Matt, following Lilah down the front path of the semi-detached house. 'Hey!' he shouted.

Lilah's step faltered but she waited until she reached the pavement before she stopped and turned on him.

'What? You could have stayed. They're your friends. You should stay.'

'I didn't want to come here in the first place,' Matt told her under his breath, in a whisper that he obviously wanted to be a shout. 'I only came here for you. If you're leaving, I'm leaving.'

Lilah searched his eyes, her chest aching.

'What do you want from me, Matt? I said I'm sorry.'

'It's not your fault.'

'Then what do you want?'

'I don't know!' Matt shouted, throwing his arms up.

Lilah recoiled a little, but his raised voice wasn't really aimed at her. He even turned away as he yelled, shouting at the street.

'Do you want to talk about it?' she asked.

'Not really.'

'Do you want me to leave?'

'No.'

Lilah sighed and folded her arms.

'Do you want to just sit together?'

Matt glanced at her and gave a shrug.

'I don't know what else to offer,' she told him.

'I don't know what to tell you,' he shouted. 'I just wish I could go back in time so none of this ever happened.'

'None of it?'

'No. Not none...' Matt sighed and then gave a little scream up to the cloudy night sky. Despite the thick clouds, it was so cold. An icy breeze blew through them and a distant thought entered Lilah's head that perhaps unseasonal snow was on the way.

'Do you want to end this?' she found herself asking, her voice breaking.

He looked up at her with wide eyes and shook his head, and she smiled, brushing away a tear that fell down her cheek.

'Well, good,' she murmured.

'No, no, no. I don't want this to end. I want there to be an us. I like us,' said Matt, rushing towards her and stopping just shy of reaching out to hold her. 'I want us. We've only just got started.'

'Yeah, and look at what happened.'

'I should have told you, I guess,' said Matt,

shaking his head. 'About how my parents are.'

'We've been together less than a week,' she told him. 'And you did tell me. I should have stopped my mum. It's just when she's excited, she likes to get things done and it's hard to stop her. But I didn't even really try to stop her, and I'm so sorry about that. I just didn't think there'd be any harm. A nice little Christmas party at the shop sounded nice. Like something Lillian would do.'

A sad smile tugged at Matt's lips, and in that moment, Lilah just wanted his arms around her. She missed his kisses, his lips on her skin, his hands on her, feeling like she was his and he was hers. They hadn't had enough of that. They hadn't had a chance.

'Lillian never met my parents,' Matt said softly.

'But she knew?'

He nodded.

'I worked so hard to get the funding for my own shop and my parents wouldn't help. They said it was a stupid dream. It took a while for Lillian to get that out of me, but when she did, she offered me the shop at a lower rate. There wouldn't be a shop if it wasn't for her, and now...' Matt swallowed hard and Lilah reached out, meaning to hug him, but not knowing how he would react. She settled for brushing her fingers over his hand. Matt didn't move.

'They just kept telling me to get a proper job. Whenever I talked about the shop, about any of my customers, they just shut down and wouldn't listen,' he said, not blinking, staring into nothing. 'That's all they do when I try and tell them about the business. They were like that when I was at school, too. Telling me to concentrate on getting good grades and to stop drawing, how that wouldn't get me anywhere. And no, they wouldn't buy me a film recorder. Not couldn't. I'd understand that. Wouldn't. They said it was silly. That there were more important things in life. That it'd be a waste of money. I wanted to go to film school. I even suggested business school, but they said no. I had to get a good pension and security.' Matt gave a bitter laugh. 'They didn't even care when the job I did get made me so miserable I couldn't get out of bed by the end of it.'

Lilah's eyes were filling with unspent tears and she blinked hard, trying to force them back, not wanting to make this about her. She took Matt's hand as he talked, stepping closer.

'I'm sorry,' she told him gently. 'I'm so sorry you went through all that. But Lillian helped. And I can help. With whatever you want. Whatever you need.' She stepped closer still and placed a kiss on the corner of his mouth.

It seemed to wake Matt up and he blinked down at her, then frowned. Her stomach somersaulted sickeningly, sending up a wave of nausea and a reminder of how hungry she was.

'You can do better than me,' he whispered.

'What?' Lilah smiled, giving a little laugh. 'No.'

'You deserve better than this.'

'No.' Her smile fell. 'I want you. I told you.'

'I don't want to drag you down.'

'You don't! You make me happy, every time I'm with you. You... you pull me up.'

'For now, but that's not how it ends.'

'You don't know that.'

'It's how it always ends.'

Lilah let the tears fall, gripping fistfuls of his coat.

'You're breaking up with me? But you said you didn't want to. I know you don't want to. Why are you doing this?'

'Because sooner or later, I'll drag you down.'

Lilah tried to search his sad eyes, but he was staring at the ground, refusing to look at her.

'What's going on?' she asked no one in particular. 'We were doing okay, we were enjoying each other, and then all of a sudden you're ending it because of what? Because of your parents?'

'No.' Matt frowned.

'Because of how they make you feel?'

Matt shrugged away from her and she let him go. Without a word, or even a look, he turned away and walked down the street.

'Where are you going?' she shouted after him.

He didn't stop, he didn't turn, but he hesitated, if only for a second.

Breathing hard, her head spinning, Lilah turned back to Danny's house to find Nat watching from the open front door. Nat held out her arms and waddled down the front path at the fastest pace she could go. A sob wrenched through Lilah as she met Nat and they hugged, Nat holding her tight.

'It's okay,' she whispered as Lilah let the tears fall. 'He'll come back. You'll see. It's all going to be okay.'

Lilah wanted to believe her, but all she could think about was Matt's back as he walked away, not even glancing over his shoulder as she called after him.

27

Danny had been messaging Matt since the Friends'
Christmas Dinner. Two days had passed and Matt
had woken on Christmas Day to yet another
message. It wasn't like Matt wasn't replying, he
was, but none of the replies seemed to satisfy
Danny. To the point where Nat had also started
messaging him.

Lilah, however, had been silent. It had occurred
to Matt to message her, but he didn't know what to
say. Every message he typed out was deleted before
he could finish a sentence.

Having got up late, Matt's father made him a
bacon sandwich for breakfast and then declared
that Christmas was done.

'I can cook dinner, if you like?' Matt offered.

'No. I don't think we'll be hungry.'

The television was occupied as his parents
caught up on crime dramas and watched the odd
piece of Christmas television. He joined them
around lunchtime, having made everyone a cup of

tea, and glanced over at his mother who had brought out her knitting needles and a ball of wool.

'I bought you presents,' he said.

When neither of his parents reacted, Matt ventured upstairs and fetched the two wrapped parcels, giving them to his parents and sitting back down.

'Oh, Matthew, you shouldn't have,' said his mother slowly, putting down her knitting.

'It's Christmas.' He shrugged. 'A time of giving and love.' He cleared his throat. 'I know you don't really want to talk,' he continued as his mother started unwrapping the gift. 'But when I went to Danny's party, I ended up having a big argument with Lilah...' He waited to see if that would stir a reaction.

'Oh? Is that relationship over before it began?'

'I hope not,' Matt said quietly. 'Although I don't know what to say to her right now.'

'Was she rude to you?'

'No. She apologised. Profusely. About the night at the shop.'

'About how rude your friend was? He should be the one apologising.'

'She apologised for organising the party.'

Finally, his mother looked up at him.

'Why would she do that?'

'Because. Look what happened.'

'That wasn't her fault.' She looked down at the present in her lap, slowly being revealed. 'It was nice to see your shop.'

'Was it?' Matt almost didn't reply, worried he might scare away this rarely seen and heard version of his mother, but also desperately wanting to hear more.

She pulled away the paper and lifted up a flat ornament, hanging on a gold chain, of glass pieces fused together to create an image of the sea, waves crashing on the beach, and the arcade and bright lights behind the sand. She looked at her son.

'You said once that Dad proposed to you there,' explained Matt. 'Where the arcade is. Lillian and Lilah's friend, Bea, made it. With Lillian, before she... before she left.' He went to ask if she liked it but bit his tongue.

'Oh.' She turned the ornament on its hanging chain, watching the light from the TV shine through it. 'He did propose to me there. It was a very windy day. If he hadn't gotten down on one knee, I wouldn't have heard him.'

Matt could hardly breathe.

'Your friend made it?' she asked.

He nodded.

'With help from Bea. She used to run an art stall at the market with Lillian. Now she's helping Lilah set up her own art business.'

'It's very nice,' said his mother, placing the ornament carefully back in its box and scrunching the wrapping paper into a ball. 'Thank you.' She went back to watching the TV and Matt sagged back in his seat. 'And tell Lilah it wasn't her fault.'

'Okay.'

'And I'm sorry we hadn't been to visit the shop before then.'

Matt froze, watching first his mother, then his father, who hadn't moved during the whole exchange.

'I don't see how you're making a career out of it,' his mother continued with a small grumble, picking up her knitting, 'but you obviously are. And it was kind of Lillian to leave you the shop.'

'It was,' Matt agreed.

His mother looked at her husband next to her on the sofa and elbowed him. 'Open your present from your son.'

His father looked down at the gift in his lap and began to unwrap it.

'Is it socks? Bit big and heavy for socks,' he mumbled. He paused as the paper fell away and then his eyes brightened and he glanced up at Matt briefly before lifting up the gift. It was a small, old-fashioned ham radio.

'Does it work?' he breathed.

'Of course it does,' said Matt. 'I got the bloke to show me how it works and I tested it a couple of times. Want me to show you?'

'I know how it works,' his father said, practically hugging the radio to him. 'Been a long time since I had one of these.'

Matt's mother gave her son a smile and went

back to her knitting.

'Why don't you call Lilah?' she asked.

'I don't know what I'd say. I ended up accidentally breaking up with her last night,' said Matt, watching his father fiddle with the radio.

'Why did you do that?'

'Because she can do better than me and I didn't want to drag her down.'

His mother lowered her knitting and stared at him.

'What on earth makes you think she can do better? You own a shop that somehow, against all logic, makes money, and she owns a flat and somehow, against all logic, is paying her bills as a wannabe artist. Sounds like you're made for each other.'

She went back to her knitting.

'Thanks, Mum. That was almost a compliment. I think.'

She didn't answer. The sound of the TV filled the room once more and Matt stared blankly at the screen, mulling over what had just happened and thoughts of Lilah.

Beside him, on the arm of the chair, his phone beeped. He looked at the screen, expecting Danny's name and instead saw Lilah's. Sitting up straight, Matt grabbed his phone and opened the message.

Come shop bad

Frowning, Matt stared at the message, trying to decipher it. Had Lilah sat on her phone and auto-correct had messaged him? Was she in trouble? Images filled his mind of her tied up in the shop, trying to message coherent sentences to him and failing as burglars ransacked the place before turning their violence on her.

Matt leapt to his feet and rang Lilah's number, holding the phone to his ear as his parents jumped at his sudden movement. His mother shook her head, frowning, as she went back to her knitting. The phone rang and rang, until it went to voicemail. Matt went to swear, then remembered where he was.

'Erm, I have to go.'

'It's Christmas!' said his mother. 'What's wrong?'

'I don't know. Lilah just sent me a strange message and she's not picking up the phone. I think something bad's happening at the shop. I need to go check.'

'Okay.'

'Take my car,' said Matt's father, gesturing to where the keys sat on a shelf in the hallway behind them. He didn't offer to help or join Matt, and his mother didn't say anything else, so Matt thanked his father, grabbed the keys, pulled his shoes on and ran out into the cold December dusk without a coat on. Heart pounding, he tried to calm his nerves enough to allow him to drive safely, although the roads were deserted. The town was never this quiet.

This was the only day you could venture out and see practically no one, and in the space between day and night, the wind blowing hard against the trees and thick grey sky, it was easy to believe the apocalypse had happened while his mother was knitting and his father was watching a crime drama.

Matt stopped at the shop, left the car on the road pulled over as he could without blocking any access, and ran to the front door.

The shop was dark and quiet, so he cupped his hands around his eyes and searched through the window. There was no one there, just the marks he'd left from his warm breath on the glass. Matt pulled out his phone again and looked up to the flat windows. The lights were on and shadows were moving. He could have rung Lilah, but there was too much adrenaline running through him. Instead, he stopped, holding his breath and when he heard a laugh come from upstairs, he pounded his fist on the front door, then rang the bell twice.

28

She'd eaten too much to be bending over going through a box of Lillian's things, so Lilah was sitting on the floor of the living room instead. It meant no bending, although her legs were already complaining about the position. Her mother was sitting on the sofa, taking things that Lilah pulled from the box. Beside her, Lilah's father watched TV, leaning back, a hand on his full stomach. They'd had to put the big light on, removing the cosy Christmas fairy light feel from the room, in order to look at the box's items properly.

The box was mostly full of art supplies and knick-knacks. Lilah put the supplies in a pile to keep and her mother chose what else she wanted to keep, the rest was put back in the box and pushed to the side. Lilah fetched another box, telling her mother about painting with Bea and her plans for the upcoming years.

'It sounds wonderful,' said Louise as Lilah lowered herself back to the floor. 'But what about paying the bills. It takes time to get a business off the ground.'

'I know. I have savings for now, and I'll start looking for a part-time job in January. Something to keep things moving.'

'Good plan.' Her mother nodded and took a notebook that Lilah handed her from the box. There was a moment of silence as they both read notebooks filled with pages of Lillian's scrawled handwriting.

'I think this is a diary,' Lilah murmured, flicking through the pages.

'So's this.' Her mother sat up straighter. 'I didn't know Lil wrote a diary.'

Soon they were consumed with what they were reading. Most of Lilah's notebook contained pages of what Lillian had painted that day, meetings with Bea, plans for the future that made Lilah's chest tighten with grief when she realised some of those plans hadn't been realised.

Then a scrawled 'Matt' caught her eye. She stopped skimming the words and sunk into the diary.

What a wonderful young man Matt is. So full of dreams and excitement. I don't understand half of what he talks about, but I love him. Do you know who else I think would love him? My lovely niece Lilah. Sometimes Matt says things and I reckon Lilah would understand him where I don't. I must introduce them sometime.

Lilah checked the date of the entry. It was from four years ago. Why hadn't Lillian introduced them? She flicked through the pages until she saw Matt's name again.

Spent the morning in the shop with Matt drinking coffee while he told me about a date he went on last night. Poor boy. It was awful! She made fun of his shop and the things he loves. I told him he was better off alone than with someone like that.

Lilah sighed, thinking of Matt's parents. At least he'd had Lillian in his corner. Her memory went back to that first meeting at Lillian's funeral and wondered, probably for the first time, what he'd really been feeling on that day. He'd lost his main supporter, Lilah realised. He must have felt so alone, and then he'd had the rug pulled under him, finding out that Lillian hadn't left him the flat. Lilah reminded herself that he had Danny, but how supportive could a friend be when that friend had a demanding career, a four-year-old and a baby on the way? Surely it was Danny who needed Matt's support at this time, but what support could Matt give if he thought he was cut off from anyone who could hold him up?

Her fingers itched to message him, but he'd broken up with her. She wanted to respect his wishes, no matter how badly she disagreed with them. How much she wanted to talk to him. She couldn't message him on Christmas Day. It could wait until he was back at work, when she could venture downstairs with a cup of coffee to see if he was willing to talk to her. As much as she wanted to talk and jump back into his arms, Lilah reckoned this would have to be a slow and patient build up to get Matt back in the relationship frame of mind. She'd have to prove herself, prove that she could be the supporter he was so desperately in need of. That she wanted to be his supporter, through all of it.

'Ah!'

Lilah and her father jumped at her mother's sudden outcry.

'What?'

'What is it?'

'Look!' her mother shouted, although she didn't offer the notebook to either of them. '"Went to Stan's today",' she read aloud, '"and painted him in the nude. He's such a fascinating man. Then we made love in his kitchen."'

She looked at Lilah with wide, happy eyes.

'Excuse me?' said Lilah. 'What else does it say?'

'Nothing! That's it. That's the end of that entry. The next entry is all about learning how to make fused glass with Bea.'

'What!' Lilah cried, trying to jump up but having to wait for the blood to return to her legs. She sat on the arm of the sofa and read the passage over her mother's shoulder. 'Were they in a relationship?'

'I don't think so. I'm sure she would have told me,' said her mother. 'Is Stanley married?'

'No, widowed. Maybe they were friends with benefits?'

'That could explain why she never told me she was sleeping with him. Or anyone, for that matter.'

'Maybe she just wanted to keep it private,' Lilah's father suggested, going back to the TV but with one eye on the notebook in his wife's lap.

'Lil? Private?' Louise looked up at Lillian's paintings on the walls around the living room. A lot of them were new, ones that Lilah had found and put up in memory of her aunt. 'Maybe. She was always the quiet one.'

'And it's always the quiet one,' Geoff murmured.

'When is this dated?' Lilah asked. They both took a moment to search for the entry's date. 'Almost two years ago,' she murmured, before returning to the floor and diving back into the box, checking the entry dates of the remaining notebooks. 'Here. Here are the next ones. See if she mentions Stanley again.' She passed another notebook to her mother and they started leafing through pages.

Geoff shook his head.

'You can't just leave her be? If she wanted you to know, she'd have told you.'

'Or written it down,' mumbled Lilah's mother, busy skimming Lillian's words. 'Here. She mentions Stanley here.' They both sat up straighter as Louise read the entry out loud. "'Went to Stan's again this evening. He made me lasagna and we drank a bottle of wine, then we painted each other's naked bodies and made love on a canvas.'"

Lilah and her mother looked up at each other with wide eyes and strained smiles.

'Haven't found that painting yet,' said Lilah.

They went back to the notebooks, Lilah skimming for Matt's name as well as Stanley's. As she turned a page, a spot of yellow appeared at the edge of the notebook. Lilah followed it carefully, turning the pages to where a single, almost fresh, yellow rose petal acted as a bookmark. Lilah glanced around the room, wondering if Lillian was watching this happen, then she read the entry the petal had marked.

Stan told me a secret today but you mustn't tell anyone.

Lilah frowned. What an odd way to put it when Lillian was writing to herself.

His daughter isn't coming back to England. He's heartbroken, of course, but he can't change her mind, nor will he go out to Australia. He told me he considers Matt his son these days, as his daughter contacts him less and less. It's so sad. I feel awful for him.

Then I mentioned that I wanted to leave my flat and shop to Matt, which led to me having to tell poor Stan about my diagnosis. He was the first I told.

I'll never forget how he held my hand.

And then he told me how he'd been considering leaving his house to Matt. Can you imagine? Maybe it means Matt won't need my flat. Just the shop. And if that's the case, I know just who to leave my flat to. But there's no knowing if Stan will change his mind, and I would hate to leave Matt in the lurch.

Let's see how this plays out.

Lilah took a deep breath and read the entry again.

'Have you found something?' asked her mother.

'No,' said Lilah, closing the notebook but leaving the petal on the page. She slid the book under her leg and delved back into the box for another notebook.

'Oh, ha!' cried her mother.

'What?'

'"I know you're reading this, Louise. I'm sorry I didn't tell you about Stan. Be kind to him. He's a wonderful man. And no, he's not married. He's widowed. Please include him. He was the best I ever found."' Louise looked up. 'She knew we'd read her diaries! That crafty, beautiful, wonderful woman.'

She laughed and Lilah joined in, until Louise's eyes went red with tears. 'Oh dear. Not again.' She grabbed a tissue from the box on the coffee table and held the notebook close to her heart.

'You keep that one, Mum,' Lilah told her, the notebook beneath her burning a hole in her leg.

Louise nodded and blew her nose, then screeched as someone banged on the front door. Lilah's heart jumped and her father leapt to his feet.

'What's that?'

'Someone at the door. It's okay,' said Lilah, standing and taking the notebook with her.

'At this time on Christmas Day?' said Louise. 'Don't answer it.'

The doorbell rang twice.

'I'll see who it is first. I'll check the peephole,' Lilah reassured her parents, pausing to put the notebook in her bedroom, hiding it under her pillow.

'No, no. I'll go. You stay here,' said her father, pushing past.

Lilah followed him down the stairs and hid behind him as he checked the peephole.

'It's Matt?' he said, turning back to Lilah.

'Matt?' Lilah pushed past her father and opened the door. 'Hey, what's going on? Are you okay?'

Matt stood on her front doorstep with

dishevelled hair, out of breath and no coat. He shivered as he looked her up and down, his breath audibly catching at the sight of the goat t-shirt she was wearing, bought from his shop. He glanced back to her father, then looked at his shop.

'What's happening?' he asked.

'I... I don't know. What's happening?' Lilah asked. 'Are you okay? You look like hell. Come in.' She stepped back to let Matt inside, but he shook his head and pulled out his keys.

'You're not in trouble?' he asked.

'What? No. Why would I be?'

'Because of the message you sent me.' Matt opened the door to his shop.

'What message?'

'And you didn't pick up when I called you.'

Frowning, Lilah pulled out her phone and checked it.

'I don't have any missed calls. I didn't hear you calling me. You didn't call me.'

Matt walked into his shop and turned on the lights, disappearing for a moment to check the shop and back room, then he reappeared, his phone in hand.

'Yes, I did. Look.'

He showed her his call log and the message she'd sent him. Lilah's father mumbled something about leaving them be, but that he'd just be upstairs, and left them to it, leaving the front door open. Lilah checked the number on Matt's phone. It was definitely hers. Her own phone had no recollection of such a message.

'This wasn't me.'

'What do you mean? Who else could it be?'

Lilah showed him her phone and their message thread, missing that vital message.

'Did you delete it?'

'I didn't even type it.'

Lilah walked into the shop and looked around. 'Everything's okay? Nothing's out of place?'

Matt joined her and looked down, then slowly slid his hand into hers. Her heart jolted, the cold from his fingers shooting through her warm body. She smiled at him, but instead of smiling back, she found him looking down. Following his gaze, they both stared at the yellow rose petal at their feet.

'Huh,' said Matt.

'Do you think Lillian sent that message?' Lilah whispered.

Matt met her gaze and she tried the smile again. This time he smiled back, squeezing her hand.

'I'm sorry I'm an idiot,' he told her gently.

She gave a soft laugh.

'You're not an idiot.' Lilah reached up with her free hand and pushed her fingers through his dishevelled hair.

'I'd like to be your idiot. If you'll have me back,' Matt told her, his eyes darting down to the petal on the floor.

'I think you'll always be my idiot,' Lilah murmured, making him look back to her with an expression that made her stomach flip. 'Dreamer,' she told him. 'You're not an idiot. You're a dreamer. And you're my dreamer. If you'll have me.'

Matt laughed.

'I'd love to have you,' he told her, kissing her just as she realised what she'd said. She laughed into the kiss and wrapped her arms around his neck, pulling him close.

'You're so warm,' he murmured into her lips.

'Come upstairs, warm up,' she said into his mouth.

'In a minute.' Matt pulled Lilah's waist closer and touched his tongue to hers, and all coherent thoughts left her.

29

JUST AFTER CHRISTMAS

Matt was running late. He ran up to his shop door, almost crashing into it. With a sandwich shoved into his mouth, found his keys and unlocked the door. Once the 'be right back' sign was down, Matt stopped, removed the sandwich from his mouth while taking a bite, and took a deep breath around his mouthful. By the time he made it to his stool behind the counter, leaning his elbows on it to finish his sandwich, Lilah was at the shop door. The bell rang out as she pushed the door open and stepped inside.

'How did it go?'

'Hmm-hmph.'

'And without the sandwich?'

Matt swallowed.

'Great. The car's full, but I ran out of time.'

'I can empty the car,' said Lilah.

'Are you sure? There's heavy stuff in there.'

Lilah thought about this a moment and then did

a little jump and clapped her hands.

'I'm just excited you're finally moving in.'

'Finally?' Matt laughed, inspecting what was left of his sandwich. 'It's barely been a month.'

'But what a month!'

Matt grinned.

'A great month.'

Lilah beamed and danced over, kissing him and then pulling a face.

'You're full of crumbs.'

'Not the first time I've heard that,' said Matt, brushing his fingers over his face and popping the last of his sandwich in his mouth. 'You know, as we're sharing the bed, we could still rent out the second bedroom.'

Lilah rolled her eyes.

'You don't want to live just the two of us?'

'It's just a waste of a room.'

When Lilah looked round to Matt, he grinned at her. She shook her head at him but couldn't hide her smile.

'Well, one day we could put a baby in there.' She smirked at Matt, and then the smirk fell when she saw his expression. He'd been lost in the thought for a moment, the idea of marrying Lilah, of her being the mother of his child, of being a father, and he found himself smiling.

Lilah gave him a strange but sweet smile, and turned to leave.

'I'm going to start bringing in your stuff from the

car. Want to help?' She opened her arms at the empty shop, and Matt sighed.

'Fine. Let me just write an "I've emptied the storage unit into my girlfriend's car and now I'm emptying that into the flat upstairs. Please bear with" note for the door.'

'Sure,' said Lilah, laughing as she left the shop.

Matt found the paper and a pen and tried to remember what he'd just said.

'Hang on, be right there,' he called as the bell over the door rang, assuming it was Lilah returning to hurry him along.

She didn't say anything, but Matt, scribbling away, sensed her approaching the counter.

'Why're you being weird?' he asked, looking up and meeting Danny's eyes.

'You're one to talk,' said Danny softly, gesturing with his head down to the baby wrapped in a soft blanket in his arms.

Letting out a gasp, Matt dropped his pen and moved around the counter to peer into the baby's face.

'Boy?' he murmured.

'Boy,' said Danny, staring proudly down at his son.

The baby was fast asleep, breathing gently, and something inside Matt gave way. This hadn't happened when Danny had shown off Rosie as a newborn. Then there had been fear, that his best friend was moving on in life without him, that one of them was now responsible for someone so small and new.

This time, that fear was still there but lessened, overwhelmed by something else.

'He's amazing,' Matt whispered to his friend. 'What's his name?'

'Lukas.'

'Lukas,' Matt repeated. 'Love it.' He put a hand on Danny's back and gave him a soft pat. 'Well done, mate.'

'While I'd like to take all the credit, I didn't do much work. This is mostly Nat.'

'Is she okay?'

'She's good. She's in the car, probably fallen asleep.'

Matt went to laugh out loud but stopped himself for fear of waking little Lukas. Behind them, the bell rang again and they both turned to watch Lilah and Nat walking in.

'Nat, you look like hell. Congratulations,' said Matt, rushing forward and gently scooping her into a hug. She put her head on his shoulder and hugged him back.

'Thanks. Don't stay here too long, I'll fall asleep on you.'

'They do say you should sleep when the baby does,' Matt told her solemnly.

Lilah had moved past him to peer at Lukas in Danny's arms.

'Where's Rosie?' Matt whispered.

'With my mum,' Nat told him. 'Getting spoiled rotten. She's a bit annoyed she has a brother and not a sister.'

'Nah, she'll come round,' said Matt. 'Once she realises how much she can torment him when he's older.'

'That's what I told her,' Nat whispered. 'But don't tell Dan I said that.'

Matt held in another laugh, watching Lilah fuss over the sleeping Lukas, wondering momentarily what their baby would look like. Would they have his eyes and her hair, or the other way around?

'He's so gorgeous, I think I just ovulated,' said Lilah.

Nat laughed.

'Whatever you do, don't smell his head then.'

Obligingly, Danny lifted the baby so Lilah could smell Lukas's head through his little yellow woollen hat.

'Oh! I had no idea babies smelt so delicious,' said Lilah, breathing him in again. 'Matt, smell the baby.'

'Yes, dear.' Matt did so happily, and perhaps the two strangers in close proximity woke Lukas, or perhaps it was Matt's loud sniffing, but soon they were met with two large, brown eyes staring up at them. Then Lukas's face wrinkled, his eyes closed, his mouth opened and a loud, piercing cry came out.

As one, Matt and Lilah stepped away.

'Oh, sure, you want to be near him when he's asleep, but the moment he cries...' said Danny, grinning and lifting his son so he could pull funny faces at the crying baby. It only made Lukas cry louder.

Eyes narrowed against the noise, Matt took another step back, glad there weren't any customers in the shop to be driven away.

'He's probably hungry,' said Nat, taking Lukas from Danny and holding him close. 'Can I feed him in here?'

'Of course,' said Matt, gesturing to the armchair. 'Do you want anything? Cup of tea? Biscuits?'

'Those the biscuits you buy for Stanley?' Danny asked.

'He won't mind.'

'I would kill for a cup of tea,' said Nat, sitting in the armchair, positioning Lukas and lifting her top.

Matt made himself busy, heading straight to the back room.

'I'll go fetch more mugs,' said Lilah, heading towards her flat.

She soon joined Matt in the back room, where the kettle had just boiled.

'I realise giving Nat the armchair in the window probably wasn't the best thing?' Matt said as Lilah entered.

She shrugged.

'She seems happy there. It's very comfortable. The baby is happy, too.'

'That's good.' Matt glanced sideways at Lilah as he poured the water into the four cups. 'I know we've only been together a month, and for all we know we'll hate living together and break up in another month, but if we don't, if we stay together...'

'Yeah?' Lilah smiled, leaning her head on Matt's free arm.

'I want one of those.'

'A biscuit?'

'A baby!'

Lilah grinned and kissed his arm through his jumper.

'I'll see what I can do.'

He looked down at her.

'Do you want one?'

'Maybe. One day.' Lilah turned her head to meet his eyes. 'It'd be an adventure, right?'

'Right.' Matt kissed the top of her head.

'I want adventures with you,' Lilah told him, taking two of the cups of tea and leaving the back room before he could reply.

Body light, chest full of love, Matt picked up the other two cups and started to walk out of the back room, just as there came a tapping noise behind him. Glancing back, Matt laughed at the sight of a yellow rose petal by the kettle.

'Hi, Lil,' he whispered. 'Look at what you went and did.'

30

THREE YEARS LATER

'I was thinking,' said Matt as they walked in through the flat's front door and paused to remove their coats and shoes. Outside, the December day was turning to dusk, darkness sweeping down the road. 'We should hold the Friends' Christmas Dinner this year. Can't be easy for Danny and Nat to do it with a seven- and three-year-old, it was bad enough with a six- and two-year-old. Maybe they could get a babysitter and just come here and have a breather.'

Lilah was already walking up the stairs to the flat, where she switched on the Christmas tree lights and collapsed on the sofa. On the windowsill, the vase that usually contained yellow roses was empty. The last roses had died and been put on the compost heap in the garden. She needed to buy more.

'That's what you've been thinking?' she called, not knowing how far Matt had gotten up the stairs.

He appeared beside her and plonked down on the sofa, putting an arm around her and lying his head back.

'Yep.'

'You haven't been thinking about what just happened? You were silent the whole way home.'

That silence from the car journey reappeared in their living room, now decorated with paintings by Lillian and Lilah. The furniture had been replaced over the years with items that Lilah and Matt had bought together, including the brand-new blue sofa they now sat on.

'I've been thinking about it,' came Matt's voice as he stared up at the ceiling.

'And?'

'It's not real.'

Lilah looked at him and then snuggled up against him, resting her head on his chest.

'I know what you mean. But it is real. It's happened. It's happening. And it's good news, isn't it?'

Matt didn't reply for the longest time, enough that Lilah lifted her head to check he was all right.

'I miss him.'

'I know you do,' said Lilah, wrapping her arms around Matt and holding him tight. 'I do, too. But he did this for you. Stanley leaving you his house was because he thought of you as a son. He loves you.'

Matt only nodded and swallowed hard, his

Adam's apple bobbing as his head was still bent back on the sofa.

'I'd rather have him back.'

Lilah pressed her cheek against Matt's chest.

'That's how I felt about Lillian. I'd rather have had her back, but I couldn't have that. Instead, she left me this incredible gift. The flat, but also you.' Lilah kissed Matt's jumper. 'And look how that turned out! Now Stanley's left you his house. Just think what amazing things he's giving you through that one act.'

'He has a daughter,' Matt whispered. 'It's bad.'

'It's not bad. You heard the solicitor. Stanley said in his will that his daughter didn't want the house, that she'd only sell it.'

'It should be hers to sell.'

'It was his to give to who he wanted. Just like Lillian's shop was hers to give to who she wanted.'

'Yeah, I felt guilty about that, too. Although not as much.' Matt lifted his head, blinked a few times and looked down at Lilah, kissing her hair. She lifted her face and kissed his lips.

'Lillian knew what she was doing,' she murmured, sitting up and kissing him again. 'Just like Stanley did.' She sat back and searched Matt's sad eyes. The notebook Lillian had used as a diary, the one she'd written Stanley's secret from five years ago, was still in the bedroom. She'd hidden it when Matt had first moved in and kept it safe all this time. Was it time to tell their secret?

'Hang on. Stay there,' she told him, kissing him again before pushing up from the sofa and heading to the bedroom. The notebook was at the bottom of a box in the wardrobe, underneath a load of photos, which was underneath a scarf. She pulled it all out, found the notebook and headed straight back into the living room, sitting back next to Matt.

Lilah opened the notebook to the page marked by the dried and pressed yellow petal.

'What's that?' Matt sat up.

'Here. Read this.' She pointed out the passage for him and handed over the book, keeping the petal safe and out of the way.

She watched Matt's eyes reading Lillian's scrawls, then he read it again.

'I don't...'

'Lillian wrote that a couple of years before she died. I found it when I moved in, on Christmas Day, actually, right before you came knocking on the door because you got that strange message we think Lillian sent. Remember? I didn't know whether to mention it, and I didn't want to ruin anything. For all I knew, Stanley had changed his mind. Or it wasn't real. And Stanley was still here, with us. So, I didn't want to upset anything. I kept it hidden away but... Well, now seems a good time to show you.' Lilah looked down at the yellow petal in her fingers. 'Lillian used this as a bookmark.' She frowned. 'Although it wasn't dried and pressed when I found it.' She looked at the empty vase on the windowsill. 'It was fresh. How did...'

'So, Stanley's house is ours?'

'Yours,' Lilah corrected. 'It's in your name.'

'Yeah, but we'll change that. Put your name on it, too.'

Lilah's heart skipped.

It had been such a busy month, full of running a Christmas market stall with Bea every weekend, all across the region. Making and packaging the art she'd created over the year to sell, including the orders she'd had from the website Matt had made for her. There had been the flat and shop to decorate, a Christmas party to hold in the shop, where Matt's parents chatted almost happily to Danny and Lilah's parents while her sister's children played with Lukas and Rosie. Stanley's armchair had been left vacant, a reminder that he was still there with them, although his funeral had been a few months prior.

Lillian's presence had apparently dwindled away, until there was only the odd noise every now and then, usually when Matt and Lilah argued. Then, on the night Stanley had died, there had come an almighty crash from the spare room, as a box of Lillian's art supplies had somehow fallen from the chest of drawers it sat on.

All traces of Lillian's spirit had grown quiet after that. Lilah had asked if she was with Stanley, but had been met with silence. Not a cold silence, but a warm, comforting lack of someone being there because they were happy elsewhere.

Still, she'd put some of Lillian's ornaments on the Christmas tree as Matt had sat on the sofa watching football. Then, gradually, over the month, wrapped presents had appeared beneath the tree. Presents for parents, for friends, for each other, and it hadn't escaped Lilah's notice that there was a small, wrapped box under the tree with her name on it, written in Matt's handwriting. A box just big enough to contain a ring, although she didn't want to get her hopes up. It could just as likely contain earrings.

'It's a four-bed house,' Matt was saying. 'We could move in and spread out. You could have your own, proper studio. That would still leave two bedrooms. We'd be future-proof.' He glanced up at the tree. 'Get a dog, maybe a cat. We could have our family there.'

Lilah fought the urge to jump up and squeal with happiness, she managed to pack it all down into a nod.

'See. Stanley would have just left his daughter the house and money. But by leaving it to you, it's so much more. He knew that.'

'He gave us our family home,' Matt agreed, meeting her gaze.

Lilah kept her mouth shut, scared of what might come out if she parted her lips. Matt watched her a moment and she stayed still, wondering what he was thinking.

'Do you want that?' he asked quietly.

'More than you know,' she said, pressing her lips back together before anything could slip out.

In that second, Matt threw his arms up in the air and hollered a cheer. Jumping, Lilah laughed.

'You idiot. You scared me.'

He wrapped his arms around her and pulled her close. Lilah resisted and instead climbed onto his lap, straddling him and kissing him hard. 'I love you,' she whispered into his lips.

'Gonna make you my wife,' he whispered back. 'Because I love you so much. Gonna marry you and make a family with you.' He stopped kissing her and pushed back a little so he could look into her eyes. 'We'll name them Lillian and Stanley.'

Lilah barked a laugh.

'The babies or the dogs?'

Matt's eyes flashed.

'Yes.'

Laughing, Lilah kissed him again, until the kiss deepened, the laughter subsided into giggles. Lillian's notebook diary lay beside them on the sofa, the pressed yellow petal holding its page, even as the notebook, as if pushed by invisible fingers, shifted and closed itself.

But Matt and Lilah were too engrossed in one another and their future to notice.

Thank you for reading Yellow Petals At Christmas.
I hope you enjoyed Lilah and Matt's story.
If you did, please consider leaving a review
wherever you get your books to help other readers
find Lillian's trail of yellow petals.

Looking for your next romance?

Try the **Christmas At The Manor** trilogy of three novellas,

Digging The Director,

A Scottish Christmas Dream

and

Let's Skip This Christmas

by Jennifer Nice.

Find your next read at
www.writeintothewoods.com/romance